# Run It Out

by Tom Dougherty

DORRANCE
PUBLISHING CO
EST. 1920
PITTSBURGH, PENNSYLVANIA 15238

Dorrance Publishing Co
585 Alpha Drive
Pittsburgh, PA 15238
Visit our website at *www.dorrancebookstore.com*

ISBN: 978-1-6853-7132-6
eISBN: 978-1-6853-7976-6

# Run It Out

*Thank you to all who supported me through the writing of this book. I wrote the end first. Then the beginning. The middle is the hard part.*

*I am especially filled with gratitude towards my amazing wife, Sherri, for giving me a life worth living.*

*I also want to thank my wonderful children, Thom and Heather, for giving me the chance to be a parent and coach.*

*Finally, I want to remember and thank my incredible niece, Katie. She read the earliest draft of this work but did not live to see the end of it. I hope she would like it.*

# MARCH 19

Mom gave me a journal today. She said that now that I am 12, I should write down the things that happen to me. I was worried that she was going to start talking about "changes," like the really gross stuff in Health class. She just meant that it would help me remember things when I am old and have children of my own. I don't plan on having children. I don't even talk to girls unless I have to do it at school.

I don't know what to write about because I don't think anything really happens to me. I go to school (6th grade). I have a cat because Dad says he is not going to walk a dog at 6:00 A.M. in the rain. Dad says a lot of things like that. Dad says that his job is to make me a good person. I think that I am good, and if I am not, I am not going to write it down.

Mom said that I should write about my family because someday I might be famous, and people who study me will read my diary for clues about my "early upbringing." Dad says that I should let him write the entries about him so that people will understand how awesome he was. Maybe I should let the future "John historians" know about us. I won't show it to Dad.

We are not interesting. Dad is a lawyer and complains about it. He likes to watch sports but doesn't play any. He likes all of the local teams even though they aren't very good. I don't know why he does that. He is also the Assistant Coach of my baseball team. It's embarrassing, but sometimes he moves me up in the batting order.

My sister, Kelly, is 15. Mom says she is going on 30. She and Mom used to talk <u>to</u> each other all the time. Now they talk <u>about</u> each other, mostly to Dad. Dad doesn't say much to Kelly, but he does seem interested in who calls her on the phone. I also know that he has her e-mail account password, but Dad pays me $5 a week to keep the secret. Kelly pays me $5 a week to not tell Dad about her other e-mail account.

Mom used to be a lawyer. Now she has cancer.

# *MARCH 19*

*I gave John a diary today. I told him to write down important things. I want him to have something to focus on during the next few months. I know that he will think it is stupid, but he thinks that most things are stupid. "Stupid" is his favorite word. He uses it often.*

*I told him to write about his family, but that may be a bad idea. We may not be interesting enough. I'm a 45-year-old lawyer who has been battling breast cancer for three years. My son likes to play baseball and annoy his sister. I met Bill when I was 22 years old, and I haven't been with anybody since. Bill annoys me at times, but that is probably the key to our marriage. I annoy him more.*

*Kelly causes me more joy and pain than Bill and John combined. We used to be so close, but I don't know what to do for her now. She knows that things are bad. She was always sensitive, even as a little girl. She would cry when her friend's fish died or her cousin broke her arm. She has been more difficult since she turned 13. She doesn't say things are stupid. She just tells me that she hates me. My friends tell me that this is normal, but I don't like it. I used to say that to my mother, and I regret it now. Perhaps Kelly will forget that she said it after I am gone. Of course, I never forgot it after Mom died.*

# MARCH 20

I will write again since Mom says it is a good idea to get into a habit. I won't write "Dear Diary" since that is really stupid. It seems like something that Kelly would do. I'm not doing it.

Mom was really tired today. She has been sick for more than a year. I do not know exactly when she got sick because Mom and Dad don't talk about it. Sometimes, they disappear into another room and speak very softly to each other. They think that Kelly and I don't know what they are saying. We don't. We know that they are saying stuff that we aren't supposed to hear, and that is scary.

Kelly thinks that Mom is going to die. I told Kelly she is stupid. People get better from cancer all the time. The old lady who lives down the street told Mom that she beat cancer twice, and she is ancient (at least 65). Mom is only 45, so she should have at least 20 more years. Mom was always healthy before she got sick. She used to run and play softball on her law firm's team. Dad said she throws like a girl, but he was smiling when he said it, so Mom didn't get too mad.

Nothing happened today.

# MARCH 20

*Dr. Jacobs, a/k/a Dr. Doom, told me that the tests were "not promising." I asked him if they taught doctors to speak like that in medical school. "Not promising?" How about, "You're doomed in six weeks," or, "Maybe your husband should sign up for an online dating service."*

*Bill just said, "Okay. So what do we do now?" Bill is always saying things like that. He wants to be brave because he thinks that he is supposed to be. I can tell that he is terrified about losing me. He sighs a lot and just looks at me too long when he doesn't think I am watching him. I watch him all the time. I haven't taken my eyes off him since the first day of law school. He is handsome and doesn't know it. That's a good quality in a man.*

# MARCH 21

Mom and Dad seem strange. They hold hands a lot. Maybe the doctor told them that would help Mom get better. They don't really say anything about how Mom is doing. She seems really tired in the last few weeks. It must be difficult to be sick. She never used to take naps. Dad could take a nap on the floor under the kitchen table. He never has trouble sleeping during the day. He has more trouble sleeping at night. Sometimes I hear him walking around after midnight.

# *MARCH 21*

*Day 2 of the Death Sentence is pretty much like Day 1. Miserable. Bill and I have spent a lot of time sitting together holding hands. It's different than before the diagnosis. Back then, holding hands was the first sign that he wanted me that night. It was annoying. After the first year of marriage, holding hands was a waste of time. It's not like I needed to know he loved me. The fact that he came home every night said it. Now, it doesn't bother me. Well, not as much.*

*I am happy that John seems to be writing in his journal every day. I wish that I had kept one when I was 12. Then again, there isn't really anything that*

5

*I want to remember about being 12. I was awkward and shy. I was silly and laughed about stupid things with my friends. I remember when my mom took me to buy my first bra. I was excited until I realized that the saleslady had to figure out my size. Talk about the perfect way to combine being awkward and shy in a public setting with a stranger. I didn't realize that I was getting measured for the seeds of my demise. Mom told me it was an important day. Mom told me about many important days in my life—and most of them were traumatic. Handing me a box of tampons and saying, "You're a woman now," was classic Mom. I probably should tell Kelly about the important days headed her way. It would help if she would actually stay in the house long enough to speak to me.*

# MARCH 22

Mom and Dad have gone crazy. They decided they have too much stuff in the basement and the attic. I don't know why they care so much. We don't see the stuff that is kept there. I don't even know what is under my bed. Some of it is under the stairs in the basement. I don't know what is in the attic because it is dark, and I don't want to go up there. I'm not scared. I just don't want to go up there. They are really excited about the dumpster in our driveway. I am pretty annoyed because the dumpster driver dropped it off right underneath my basketball net. How am I supposed to work on my buzzer beaters with a dumpster beneath the rim? When my school loses the college championship because I brick the final shot, I hope my Dumpster Parents are happy.

# *MARCH 22*

*Dumpster Day! I ordered the dumpster two weeks ago, but it was delayed by the snow. When we moved here, Kelly was three, and I was pregnant. Even though we moved from an apartment to a house, there were things that we*

7

just carried from the truck right into the attic. Important things like law books, coats I didn't wear, suits I hated, and dresses that didn't fit.

After John was born, more things went in the attic. Kelly got a big girl bed, so her crib went upstairs. John couldn't use her crib because the "experts" said that cribs made before the year he was born were unsafe. I was stupid enough to listen to experts then. I never stopped to think that Kelly had survived the death crib.

Kelly's kitchen set. John's first bike. Bill's golf clubs. Bill's next set of golf clubs. More clothes, dresses, and coats. It was amazing what we found when we finally decided that it was time to clean house. I originally wanted to have a yard sale, but Bill threatened to buy it all from me and put in back in the attic. He said that he didn't want it to look like we needed the money. He did agree to throw it all out.

I don't think that Bill has figured it out. I know that after I am gone, Bill will never discard anything. He had trouble tossing things in the dumpster that my mother gave me because they were "family history." Even though it wasn't his history, he is weird about things like that.

We filled the dumpster to the top with the debris of two decades together. The highlights included:

* The death crib. Its reign of terror has come to an end without any blood on its slats.
* John's crib. There was no blood on it, either. That was a little surprising since he climbed/fell out of it so many times.
* John's first bike. I still remember Bill holding on to the back as John started to peddle faster and faster. John didn't even know that Bill had let go until he rode by himself for a whole minute. He was so proud that he didn't cry when he fell over. Kelly said, "So what?" because that is what older sisters do.
* The red coat. I wore it the winter that I started dating Bill. I really loved that coat, but it just wasn't in style anymore. I was tempted to save it from the dumpster until Bill told me about the mummified mouse that he found in the pocket when he brought it downstairs. I haven't been that nauseous since my last chemo treatment.

\*   *The kitchen set. Kelly loved that set. When she was four, she used to make me breakfast and lunch with her toy food, pots, and dishes. The experts say that girls need to focus on what they can accomplish as adults rather than pretend to be cooks and mothers. The experts should try spending more time with children. Kelly was sad to see it go in the dumpster, but she pretended it was no big deal.*

*It feels like the house is a little empty now that the dumpster has departed. I am sorry that I won't be around to fill the dumpster again in a few years. I know that Bill won't be able to do it.*

Dad came home late today. He said that tonight was the baseball draft. As the Assistant Coach, he had to attend the meeting with the Head Coach, Mr. Kraft. Dad and Mr. Kraft have coached together since I was nine years old. They are way too interested in selecting a baseball team. There are about 20 really good players and everybody else. Dad said that he really enjoys the draft, but he won't tell me what the other coaches say about the players. I am happy that he selected Jason for the team because he is a good pitcher. He is also fun to hang out with. His parents are divorced, so we can watch whatever we want at his house. Dad says that we have a good team.

# *MARCH 23*

*Bill came home after selecting John's baseball team. He just kept talking about the "arms" they got and the great hitters on the roster. He also told me stories about some of the things that the other coaches say about the players that are selected. There was one boy that Bill wanted to draft, but Stan Kraft refused because the boy's mother is a real bitch. She complained to Bill last year after every game because her son didn't bat first or didn't pitch or played too many innings in the outfield. Bill never blew up at her, but I heard about it after every game. John will be happy that Jason is on his team, but I am not thrilled. I think that he is a bad influence, especially since his parents got divorced. I prefer to have Jason at our house because I don't know what goes on when he is at his dad's house. From what I heard, his dad had more girlfriends after he got married than before.*

# MARCH 24

Mom showed me a lot of pictures today. There were too many pictures of Kelly. Mom said parents take more photos of the first child. Dad said Kelly was just cuter and started laughing. Dad says a lot of things like that. I liked looking at the pictures. Mom told me stories about each one. I don't know how she remembers so much stuff.

I told Jason that he is on my team, but he has to keep it a secret until Mr. Kraft sends out an e-mail to all the players. He probably has already told everybody that he is on my team. He thinks he is the greatest player ever. Dad says he could be really good if he tried hard. I don't think that Dad likes him very much.

# *MARCH 24*

*We found a bunch of photos when we were getting ready for Dumpster Day. John wanted to know why there were more photos of Kelly than him. I told him the first child usually gets photographed more. I didn't tell him that the second child with strained peas on his face or sleeping on a stuffed animal isn't as interesting. I also didn't tell him that we were too exhausted and too busy to take pictures. I hope he knows that he was loved just as much.*

*There were so many pictures and so many memories.*

\* *Sullivan Hall Freshman year. It was so weird to look at this picture. Every girl was 18 and full of life (and beer). I don't know why big hair was so popular. Kelly asked me if perms were required back then. I liked mine at the time and thought it looked sexy. I shouldn't say it, but I looked good. I used to think that I needed to lose weight then. Two children later, I would not mind getting back to that body without* *running and going to a gym. I guess the chemo did have the benefit of weight loss.*

*The 10 girls in the picture are still my friends, but I don't see or speak to them very often. Two of them became doctors, and three are lawyers. Eight are moms, and two of them started dating each other after college (or before graduation, but I never believed those rumors at the time). Three are divorced, and Allison should be. Jane died of cervical cancer two years ago. Her funeral was terribly sad. I hope the girls will be able to attend mine. I should tell Bill about the lesbians. That should brighten his mood.*

\*  *Spring Formal Junior Year. I loved that black dress. My date was a friend, Dave. Bill asked if it was a serious relationship. I told him that it was only serious for about an hour. I don't think he liked that answer, but anything that happened before I met him does not require an explanation or apology. I remember that it was a really fun night. All of my sorority sisters were there, even Jane, who had a black eye from playing softball. She still looked good (maybe I should have been a makeup artist instead of a lawyer). The dinner was at a hotel in the city. I think there was food. I know the margaritas were strong.*

*We all stayed really late and the party didn't end until they shut down the bar. I know that a bunch of us went to Dave's fraternity. As long as you made it home before the sun came up, it was not the walk of shame. It was close.*

*Dave became an architect and married a pediatrician. I heard that they have six children, which is more than the number of hairs on his head. Or mine.*

\*  *Law school softball. I met Bill the first day of law school. We met at the Dean's Reception before classes started. He told me that his brother, Jack, suggested that he introduce himself. I can't believe that Jack was so stupid, especially after he broke up with my roommate at her sister's wedding the summer before law school started (he should have waited* *until the next day because she really was a bitch). After Jack intervened, I gave Bill another chance. I never dated anybody else. I think that he still owes me a first date since we never left my apartment that night (LA Law was on).*

*The softball game between the students and the professors was a big deal (to the professors). Somehow, Bill talked his way onto the student team even though he wasn't very good. He used to joke later that he was a switch-hitter because he could strike out from both sides of the plate.*

*In the picture, Bill is at the plate with a stance that would get John yelled at by Coach Dad. I was drinking beer near third base. Bill scored later that inning when he collided with Professor Anderson at home plate. She dropped the ball, but Bill received a C+ in her Contracts class, so I don't know who really won that battle.*

\* *First weekend away. We were law students, so we didn't have money to go anywhere exotic on our first romantic weekend away. I remember that we found a boarding house in Ocean City, New Jersey. When Bill asked the 200-year-old woman who owned the place ("Dot") if there were rooms available, she said she did not rent by the hour, and that we would have to pay for the entire night. Bill said that we would take the room and that he would sleep on the floor. After we spent the night on the worst mattress in the world, Bill said that he would have preferred the floor. This was the trip when I fell in love with him. When I told him that, Bill said it took me long enough—he loved me as soon as he saw me. True or not, I never get tired of hearing it.*

# MARCH 25

Mr. Kraft sent out the e-mail to the team introducing himself as the Head Coach. He said he was happy to be the coach and wanted the players to have fun. Coaches always say that. I bet that coaches didn't have fun when they lost as players. Mr. Kraft never yells at the players, but he does seem to turn red when we do stupid stuff on the field. Dad also sent out an e-mail to the team introducing himself. Dad always does things like that. It is stupid.

Dad gave me my hat for the season. We are the Dodgers. Dad said that he doesn't know why he always gets stuck with a team name that he hates. Since Dad hates every team that is not the Phillies, it happens every year.

# *MARCH 25*

*Bill gave me a Phillies hat today. I decided to start wearing a baseball hat since the wig gets hot and itchy. Bill said that I looked sexy (he always used to try to get me to wear baseball hats because they were "hot"). I said that he must like skinny bald chicks with scars. He said his secret was out. He has a way of making me laugh.*

*Bill told me that Stan sent out the e-mail to the players. It introduced him and Bill as the coaches and said the feel-good stuff about having fun and playing hard. Yawn. I would have told them to play hard and try to win because losing sucks, and you might as well win because it gives you something to think about when you are dying. Perhaps that is a bit dark. It's probably better that I am not a coach. Kelly never wanted me to help with her softball teams because she said I got too excited. That is unfair. I was only asked to leave one game. That girl was definitely out at home.*

# MARCH 26

Jason told me that he thought that my Dad's e-mail was unnecessary and stupid. I wanted to agree with him, but somebody has to stick up for Dad sometimes.

## *MARCH 26*

*Bill was annoyed that the parents of half the boys on the team have not responded to either of the e-mails sent out by the coaches. I suggested that it was possible that not everybody checks their e-mail every 10 minutes like he does. However, the level of rudeness of some parents is pretty high. They act like Bill is their employee rather than a volunteer coaching their son. I don't think that he needed to send a second e-mail, but Bill tends to do things like that. I don't know why. I stopped trying to figure that out years ago.*

# MARCH 27

*This afternoon, I tried to access my firm's website, so I could review the status of some of my cases. I "tried" because Bill decided yesterday to install a program on the computer that he claimed would make it more convenient for me to work from home.*

*I gave up after five attempts and seven apologies from Bill. I know that he means well. Bill is obsessed with "improving" the television and computer. John and Kelly hate watching anything with him because he usually can't avoid adjusting the picture or sound for more than half an hour. He also changes channels every time there is a commercial to see if something better is on. Bill's definition of "better" usually involves an obscure eighteenth century battle or a pirate.*

# MARCH 27

I didn't write much yesterday because nothing happened. Nothing happened today. I guess that the future John historians will have to leave these dates blank in my story.

# MARCH 28

*I was able to get the computer working after two calls to the office tech support guy. When I called him, he asked what Bill had done this time. I told him that Bill was making our system work better, and he just laughed. This was not the first time that Bill had generated this kind of phone call.*

*I started going through the e-mails that have backed up for the past week. I always find it amusing that the people who never respond to my phone calls and e-mails hunt me relentlessly when they decide that they have something important to discuss.*

# MARCH 29

*I got an e-mail from one of my clients about making "subtle changes" to a release for a settlement that I reached a few weeks ago. That term, "subtle changes," brought me back to a better time before the darkness fell.*

*A few days after I underwent my yearly mammogram, my doctor's receptionist called and left a message that there were "subtle changes" detected compared to the prior year's film. "Subtle changes" are cutting your bangs or highlighting your hair. "Subtle changes" are new towels in the bathroom or letting Bill approach me from the other side of the bed. I didn't know that subtle changes in my left breast would lead to biopsies, lumpectomies, and removal of the whole damn thing. I certainly didn't expect the message to come from a receptionist. I deserved at least a secretary to deliver the news.*

# MARCH 30

I forgot to write anything yesterday because nothing happened. Today was our first practice. We had to stand in a circle and say our name, grade, and where we go to school. I hate that. We all know each other. Dad says it helps the coaches "get to know the players." I don't think Dad knows the players until we get our uniforms, and he writes down the numbers.

Coach Kraft said he is happy to have so many pitchers, but anybody who wants to pitch will get a chance. Me and Jason are the best pitchers, but there are rules on how many pitches we can throw, so we need more than us. Dad said all the coaches were talking about Abby Taylor as a pitcher, but Coach Kraft was "old school" and would not draft a girl.

# MARCH 30

*I felt a little tired today but pushed through it. Bill said the "team is looking good." Bill has said that after the first practice of every team that John and Kelly were on. The Trophy Case (the mantle above the fireplace) is still empty.*

# MARCH 31

*During Dumpster Day, I found my address book. I remembered getting it in eighth grade from my mom. This was long before people had cell phones. I don't even know John and Kelly's numbers. I only remember Bill's number because we used to only have one cell phone, and he kept it when I got mine several years later. Bill is not a fan of new things. We still have a landline "in case of an emergency" or if the cell phones "go out." If all of the cell phones go out, who is he going to call? Even 911 will probably not answer the call because they probably think that anybody who still has a landline is a hoarder with 15 cats and piles of* Time Magazine *ready to fall and trap the rescuers.*

*It was fun to go through the entries – in different color ink depending upon their importance:*

* *Rachel (Green) – Seventh grade. I remember going to her Bat Mitzvah. We got to dress up in fancy dresses and sprain our ankles wearing our mothers' high heel shoes. She was really nervous to read from the Torah. I thought she did a great job, but I didn't speak Hebrew, so I wouldn't have known any better.*
* *Bruce (Pink) – Seventh grade. He was my first major crush. He had perfect hair and a perfect smile (without braces!). I used to write his initials intertwined with mine on my notebook during Spanish class. We stayed "just friends" during high school. On the last day of school,*

*he signed my yearbook and wrote, "Too bad we won't be at the same college next year." What?!? If this was an eighties movie, he would have driven to my house and kissed me while I was reading my yearbook. But he went on vacation to Spain right after graduation, and his parents moved later that year. I heard that he is a Spanish teacher. And bald. Such a loss.*

* *Mary (Purple) – Eleventh grade. She was my savior in math and science class. She was the smartest person I ever met. Her fake ID cards were perfect. I owe many of the stupid things I did in high school to her. I would like to talk to her again, but I think she went to work for the CIA.*

* *"The First Guy" (Red) – He was my "first" in college. Also my "second" and "third." Possibly "fourth," but it was Senior Week after too much Mad Dog 20/20. We were absolutely wrong for each other except when we were occasionally "together." Bill wonders why, if we were so absolutely wrong for each other, that I kept updating his phone number and e-mail in my book. I don't know. Do they even still sell Mad Dog 20/20? Bill always thinks this guy was so special. Maybe he can date him when I'm gone.*

# MARCH 31

Mom gave me an address book. Great. A new assignment. I am trying to keep up with the journal. Mom said it is a good idea to keep phone numbers and e-mails in a safe place in case I lose my phone. If I lose my phone, how am I going to call anybody? She said I could use the phone in the kitchen. We have a phone in the kitchen? Mom also said to not have too many cats. She is so weird.

# APRIL 1

Abby Taylor told me that she was traded to my team for Jason. I was really mad because he is my friend, and she is a girl. Then she started laughing and said it was an April Fool's joke. Maybe it would be a good trade, but I won't admit that to her.

# *APRIL 1*

*I waited all day for Dr. Jacobs to call and tell me that my cancer diagnosis was just a really bad April Fool's joke. He didn't call.*

*Bill did not play any tricks on me on me today. Maybe he knows that I am not feeling up to jokes as the curtain comes down; or he wants to keep me nervous that a trick is coming. However, he is the worst at keeping secrets or waiting for anything. I am surprised that he hasn't given me my birthday and Christmas presents in case I don't make it.*

# APRIL 2

*Bill got me. When I went downstairs, the kitchen was filled with balloons. I couldn't get in to get my coffee, and he knows that is dangerous. When I popped enough balloons to get my coffee, I called him to ask why he did it. He denied it at first but then started laughing. He said that I was doing too much work/housework and needed to rest. He thought it would slow me down. He ran out of balloons before he could fill the living room.*

*Today is Good Friday. When I was growing up, my parents made us give up candy for Lent. After I went to college, I did not give up anything. There was a time when Bill was really irritating me, and I threatened to give him up for Lent, but we were "trying."*

*I went to church with Bill. We usually take (drag) John and Kelly, but it just didn't seem worth the fight this year with so many other things going on. I am not the most religious person, but the story of the crucifixion really hit home today. I certainly would not compare what I went through to being nailed to a cross, but Jesus did not go through surgery and months of radiation and chemotherapy, either. As soon as I had that thought, I realized it was probably not a good idea to piss off God this close to meeting Him.*

*When I told Bill about my thought, he just said, "You know, they actually put the nails through the wrists and used ropes to tie the arms to the cross. The victim actually suffocated when they could no longer support their weight." Why does he know this stuff?!?*

# April 2

Dad filled the kitchen with balloons, so I could not get breakfast today. He gave me a Snickers bar and said it was the breakfast of champions. Kelly never eats breakfast.

Today is Good Friday. Dad said Kelly can't go out with her friends tonight because it would not be appropriate. I don't think God really cares, but I don't want to fight with Dad. I don't think Mom really cares because she does not want to fight with Kelly. They fight a lot.

# APRIL 3

We had practice today. Dad made us work on stealing bases. He said we had to slide feet first, or the umpire will call us out. It is to protect our head. That is stupid. Safe is safe. Dad said that rules are rules. I think it was another life lesson.

# *APRIL 3*

*I went shopping today. I had to buy candy for the Easter baskets. Kelly always talks about her weight, but she is addicted to peanut butter and chocolate. One day won't make a difference, and it will all be gone in one day. John just wants chocolate. He thinks it is funny to bite the bunny's butt first and then the ears. I always buy them jellybeans and marshmallow chicks even though they hate them. If I just happen to eat what is left over, it is not my fault.*

*When I grew up, Mom always cooked a ham for dinner. I hate ham. I never understood why it was popular at Easter. Jesus was Jewish. We can have chicken tomorrow. Hamburger Helper does not have a Resurrection flavor.*

# APRIL 4

*Happy Final Easter. Good job, Jesus. Tell Death to suck it. I never really thought about Heaven when I was growing up. I just assumed I was going. Now I am not so sure. I think I lived a good life. Just not enough of it. I have no idea what happens after you die. I hope that it has wine and jellybeans. Hell? I've already lived it.*

*John and Kelly enjoyed their baskets. I was a little annoyed when Kelly ate two marshmallow chicks and John ate some jellybeans. Rules are rules!*

# APRIL 4

Mom gave us our Easter baskets. She used to claim that the Easter Bunny brought them. That is stupid. Why would a bunny bring baskets of chocolate bunnies to children to eat? Creepy. I tried some jellybeans. They were okay. I saw Mom staring at me when I was eating them. She looked mad.

# APRIL 5

*I found our Wills today. I wanted to review mine and make sure everything is "in order" to be sure Bill doesn't screw anything up. I had a higher grade in Wills, Trusts, and Estates class. It was the most boring class in school. Of course, we hired somebody else who actually liked writing wills. Strange man but very skilled. Our wills are very simple. If I die first, everything goes to Bill and "the First Guy," so they can start a life together. Just kidding. Everything goes to Bill. If Bill dies before me, I have already planned my alibi.*

*We also prepared Power of Attorney and Living Will forms. That allows one spouse to make decisions for the other spouse if they are unable to decide for themselves. This means that if I am unconscious, Bill can make decisions about my care. If I am on life support, he can decide to turn off the machines. He promised that he would if he thought I was suffering. As I get closer to my end, I am worried that he may never let me go, Maybe I should have chosen Kelly. She would let me go if I suffered a broken fingernail.*

# APRIL 5

Mom finished all of my jellybeans. School is so boring. We are supposed to have practice this week. Jason said that he can't go because he has to see a dentist about getting braces. That sucks. I hope that I don't need braces. Abby Taylor just got hers and said they suck.

# APRIL 6

*I started thinking about who I want to see in Heaven. Mom and Dad, of course. I wonder if my dad will know me. Even though he was the reason I was named Jennifer, he had dementia and did not know who I was for the last year of his life.*

*My freshman roommate, Jane, who died from cervical cancer. She was so smart and funny. When she passed away, we all said she was a "warrior" without knowing what it really meant. Now I know it means getting up each day until you can't, so you don't make your family sad. She was always optimistic and would talk about what she planned on doing when she got better. She didn't get to do any of it. Which sucked because I really wanted to ride camels with her, George Clooney, and Brad Pitt in Egypt.*

*My first boyfriend, Joe? Maybe. We dated in eleventh grade. I remember that he was always telling jokes. He had long hair, which my dad hated but my mom liked, and played guitar. Everybody wanted to be his friend. Especially other girls. That's why we did not date in twelfth grade. He killed himself in college. All the jokes and songs hid a very deep sadness that I did not see. I always blamed myself for not seeing it. I need to ask him if he wished he could go back to just before he jumped and stop himself. I am afraid he might say, "No. You would not have been there anyway."*

# April 6

We had an assembly today. They brought all the sixth graders together. I thought that it was going to be about "changes." That is so gross. Instead, they had a speaker talk about her life. She told funny stories and how she had fun with all of her friends. Then she said that one day she did not want to live anymore. It was very quiet. She said that it is normal to be sad or feel like nobody understands you and you can't fix anything. She said that if we ever feel like that, we need to talk to somebody like our parents or a teacher or a doctor. She did, and now she wants to help other people.

# APRIL 7

*Snow day! This was completely unexpected. It was supposed to just be cold and rainy today. John and Kelly were excited to have the day off. Bill was mad because he was supposed to have practice today. He would have gone ahead, but Mr. Kraft said that eight inches of snow was too much. Bill said it would make sliding drills more fun. He was serious.*

*Bill was excited to use the snowblower. He disappeared for hours. I thought that he finally run away or got lost in the snow. He told me that he cleared our driveway. Then our neighbors' driveways. Then the sidewalk to both ends of the street. If he had not run out of gas, he might still be going.*

*I was supposed to see Dr. Jacobs today but cancelled because of the weather. It's just as well. He never has good news. So we went sledding!*

*Our town has a great park with three hills for sledding. Not as good as sliding down hills in college on trays "borrowed" from the dining hall, but I gave up day-drinking 20 years ago. I went down the hill with John and Kelly and then just watched them. They looked happy together. When they were younger, they did a lot of things together. Well, John did what Kelly told him to do, but they were happy. Of course, that changed when he was about eight and she acted like she was 30. A good day.*

# APRIL 7

Snow day! It was so cool that we got a day off today. Dad wanted to still have practice. I think he was mad that Coach Kraft cancelled it. Dad is just crazy.

# APRIL 8

*Slush day! I am sore from sledding, but it was better than the pain and sore-*
*ness of the last few years. The snow is melting quickly. Bill said that it was*
*due to the angle of the sun. I may have married the most boring man on Earth.*
*But he can be funny, too. He sometimes sings along to the radio and changes*
*the lyrics. When we first started dating, we went to a club with some of my*
*college friends. Bill went over to the DJ. He said that he dedicated a song to*
*me. I thought it was really sweet. Then I heard the DJ say, "This one goes out*
*to Jen!" It was "I Touch Myself" by the Divinyls. I almost died. So did Bill,*
*but I couldn't stop laughing.*

# APRIL 8

Today in Health class, we learned about strange feelings and not to be
ashamed of our bodies. Gross. The teacher asked if we had any questions. Who would talk about that stuff? Gross.

# *April* 9

*I went to the library today with John. I have not taken Kelly in years. I think the last book she read was* Where the Wild Things Are. *Since I am not really working, I have time to read. I have always loved reading. I read every night until it is time to sleep. Sorry, Bill. I realized that although I read several different authors, I essentially read three books over and over:*

* *Sisters discover that their mother or father or grandparents had a deep secret that threatens to tear their world apart. One sister drinks too much or does drugs. The other sister is a journalist/detective/ author/whatever who unravels the mystery and meets…the sister they did not know about!*
* *A dog dies and goes to Heaven and meets other dogs he used to know. Or an author dies and meets his dogs and the pets of other dead people who are walking their dogs in Heaven.*
* *A woman with a mysterious past moves to North Carolina. Or Martha's Vinyard. Or Nantucket. When she settles in, she finds love with a man or woman with a dead wife. Just as they are falling in love…her unknown sister shows up asking about her real mother!*

*Can't get enough of those. I took out several books. The librarian said they were due back in 30 days. I made no promises.*

# April 9

Mom took me to the library today. I need to do a book report on a famous person. My teacher said that it had to be somebody who changed history. That is pretty broad. She also gave us a list of people we could not write about – George Washington, Abraham Lincoln, Martin Luther King, Jr., or 10 other dead people. Still pretty broad. I decided to write about a baseball player named Jackie Robinson. He was the first black player to play on a team with white players in major league baseball. I did not believe that people were so stupid back then. If a person can play, they should play.

# APRIL 10

We had a scrimmage today. This is our last practice before we start the season. We played hard to win, but it didn't really matter. Sometimes the coaches would have us replay a situation again. Sometimes we would start an inning with a runner on base, so we could work on pitching and defense while the other team worked on base-running and offense.

# APRIL 10

*John and Bill had their final practice today. It was a scrimmage, so it did not count in the standings. Bill told me that several times during the game, they would redo a play, so the players could fix their mistakes. I wish real life was a scrimmage. I would like to correct a few errors.*

*I would have tried to help my high school boyfriend get treatment if I had known he was depressed. After suicide, everybody who saw nothing blames themselves for not seeing what they could not have seen.*

*The First Guy would not have been my first and might not have ever earned a number. I don't know who would have been first, but it probably would not have been Bill. He always wondered if he was the best. I thought the fact he was the last answered that question, but men just think differently.*

*I would not have kept delaying that mammogram. I pushed it off for trials, vacations, the flu, Kelly's field trips, John's field trips, etc. When Bill finally pushed me to go, it was...The one time I knew Bill was right, and I ignored him for too long.*

# APRIL 11

The book on Jackie Robinson is really good. He had to deal with a lot of mean stupid people just to play baseball. Dad said things were really bad for black people, but he showed great courage. I asked him about what things were like when he was growing up. He did not recall any incidents of violence or calling people bad names, but he grew up in a very white town. I asked Mom, and she said the same as Dad.

# *APRIL 11*

*John is really interested in his book on Jackie Robinson. He asked me about race relations when I was growing up. I told him that I never really thought about it because there were so few black people in my town. I used to watch shows like* Good Times *and* What's Happening? *and never really thought about the characters being black. I just thought that the shows were funny. I said that there have always been stupid people, but he should just try to be fair to everybody. Probably not a great answer, but it's honest.*

# APRIL 12

I finished my book report. I usually hate writing them because it is usually a boring topic, but I learned a lot. I hope I get a good grade.

# APRIL 12

*I finished one of my books today. It was so good. The sister who was a lawyer found out that her mom had another child when she was 16. That child was adopted by a couple in North Carolina. When she was 17, she was drunk and killed the wife of a handsome man in a traffic accident. The sister who was a lawyer met the handsome man, and they got married and moved to Martha's Vineyard!*

# APRIL 13

*John got an A+ on his book report. He was very excited. He has always been a good student, but he really tried hard on this assignment. I wish Kelly tried harder. She used to be a solid A student. When she got to high school, her grades started to slip. She got involved in clubs and activities, and I know that is important, too. I just want her to live up to her potential. Then again, I lived up to my potential and beyond. I still got cancer. Maybe I should have joined more clubs.*

# APRIL 13

A+! My teacher said my book report was very well written. She could tell that I was really interested in the topic. I want to read more about Jackie Robinson and other players.

# APRIL 14

*Today is our twentieth wedding anniversary. I know we vowed to stay together in sickness and in health, but nobody thinks it will apply to them. Sickness is supposed to be the flu or a broken foot. Maybe a mild heart attack for Bill, but not THIS.*

*We were married the year after law school. We both had jobs that paid the bills. Barely. We were young and thought we would someday be rich. Or at least doing better than barely paying the bills. We wanted children and thought that we would be great parents. Are we? I would ask John, but he would just say yes to get away. I would ask Kelly, but she would be too honest.*

*Bill made reservations at the restaurant where we ate before he proposed. He was so nervous then. We had discussed marriage over the past two years but wanted to wait until at least after the Bar Exam in August. That was the most stressful time in our lives before we knew what real stress was. When dinner was over, I waited for the big moment. Nothing. After dessert – nothing.*

*After leaving the restaurant, we started walking back to our apartments. We did not live together at that point because Bill said it would kill his mom. The vodka and cigarettes took care of that years later. I started wondering if my address book was up to date and who I could call when I dumped Bill. Then a man driving a horse-drawn carriage pulled up next to us and asked if I was Jen. When I said yes, he told us to get in the carriage. I first thought that this was a unique way to be kidnapped, but I was mad at Bill, so I didn't care.*

*When I turned to look back at Bill, he was on one knee. Until he fell over because carriages are bumpy rides. He tried and fell over again, so I told him to sit. He sat across from me and proposed. It was perfect.*

*We talked about that night over dinner. Bill said that he tried to find the same driver to recreate our ride, but he could not remember his name. He did remember the horse was named Omar, but that was not enough information. He told me that horses can live 30 years, so he will start planning for our twenty-fifth anniversary. We laughed but knew that this was unlikely. Horses must retire, right?*

# APRIL 14

Mom and Dad went to dinner for their wedding anniversary. They have been married 20 years. That is a very long time. Dad asked me to see if I could find a horse named Omar in Philadelphia. Stupid.

# APRIL 15

*Tax Day. At least there is one thing I won't miss. I am in charge of filing our taxes because Bill hates forms. It's not like I love them. It's just that he agonizes over every question like it's an essay. Number of Dependents? "Does that count Kelly when she says she hates us and can't wait to move out?" Other income? "Does that include the $11.50 left over in the team snack fund, and Bill Kraft said to keep it?" Yes and no. If I did everything right, we will receive a small refund. Or Bill will receive it. I don't know when the check will go out; or when I will check out.*

# APRIL 15

Our Social Studies teacher talked about taxes today. She said that taxes are the way that the government can pay for things like the military and highways and helping poor people. Dad is mad when he talks about the government. He says that I am lucky that I don't have to pay taxes. I only make $10 a week because of Kelly's e-mails.

## APRIL 16

*John had a dance at school tonight. I don't think John even realized it was supposed to be a dance. He is such a boy. Bill drove him to the school and told him to not hurt himself because they have their first game tomorrow. What did Bill think John was going to do at a dance? Play basketball or just run around with his friends?*

## APRIL 16

Tonight was fun. All of the sixth graders got to play in the gym from 7:00 to 10:00. The girls called it a dance, but they only danced with each other. And Jason. The boys played basketball and just goofed around. There was pizza and snacks in the cafeteria. Kelly asked me if I kissed Abby Taylor yet. She is so stupid. Abby Taylor was with the girls most of the night, but she did play basketball for a few minutes. She is really good. Even wearing a skirt.

# APRIL 17

*John and Bill were supposed to have their first game today. It was cancelled because it was raining...since yesterday. Bill never thinks a field is too wet to play. He says that none of the players weigh more than 100 pounds, so they won't sink into the mud anyway. He actually drove with John over to the field while it was raining. When they came back, I asked Bill why he was limping. He said he slipped because the pitching mound was "a little wet."*

# APRIL 17

We did not play today because it rained. And rained. Dad always thinks it will stop raining in time for a game or that the field "isn't that bad." He drove by the field at game time to see if it was playable. He walked out to the pitcher's mound and slipped on the mud. I think he hurt his knee but he said the field was "okay."

# APRIL 18

Our first game is tomorrow. Our game was rained out yesterday. We are playing the Phillies. I know that Dad wishes that our team had that name. He told me that he could have traded for the name with Mr. Murphy at the draft but that he would have had to trade me and my friend, Jeff. He said that the team really needs Jeff, so the price was too high. Then he laughed. Dad makes a lot of jokes like that. He must think that it is funny. It isn't. Jeff can't pitch. I can.

# APRIL 18

*Dr. Jacobs told me that the treatment isn't working "as well" as he hoped. If it isn't working as well as he hoped, then it sure as hell isn't working as well as I hoped. I am trying to be positive, but it's really difficult. I am tired by the afternoon. I know that I am losing weight. Great. I am finally losing the weight left over from carrying Kelly and John.*

*Bill told me that "we" will be fine. I know that he is trying to be positive, but I may have to stab him if he keeps talking about "us" and "we." I find it hard to believe that I am being told to have a positive attitude by a man who doesn't speak for two days if the Eagles lose a game.*

*On a brighter note, John has his first game tomorrow. I know he is excited, but he won't show it. He doesn't like to admit anything is exciting. Bill does not have that problem. He has been talking about the game plan and the line-up for the last three days. He and Coach Kraft are on the phone more than Kelly and her friends. I asked Bill what they could possibly talk about every day. He said "baseball and the players' moms." I may need to get out the knife sooner than I thought.*

# APRIL 19

We won our first game 11-10. I started the game as catcher. I almost threw out two runners, but Dan dropped the ball both times. Dad said Dan probably won't be at second base too often this season. I like when Dad tells me the secret coaching stuff. He told me that I am not allowed to tell the players these things. I won't tell Dan he sucks at second base because I think he knows it.

I pitched the last two innings. Coach Kraft brought me in with the bases loaded and two outs in the fifth inning. The first batter hit a pop up to Dan. He can't catch pop ups, either. Two runs scored. The next batter hit a line drive to me, and I caught it. I struck out three batters the next inning, and we won.

Mom was at the game. She was wearing a Phillies hat, which was embarrassing because we were playing the Phillies. Dad offered to let her wear his Dodgers cap, but she said it was okay. I think that she knows that Dad likes to wear the team's cap as a coach. He is so weird about it. He even writes "Coach Fitzgerald" inside it.

Kelly came to the game. I bet that she doesn't even know I won. She spent the whole game talking to Jason's brother. Stupid.

# APRIL *19*

*John and Bill won today. Bill gets so nervous when John pitches. I never worry about it because I know he can get the job done. John would not have given up any runs except that one of the boys on his team can't catch anything. Anything. His mother is really nice, and I was sitting next to her during the game, so I didn't say much when he was trying to blow the game.*

*I wore the Phillies hat that Bill gave me. He offered to let me wear his hat since he was worried that I was wearing the opposing team's hat. He said that it was a violation of baseball rules to appear to support the other team. I told him he was crazy. He knows it. I appreciated the offer, but I knew that he wanted to keep his cap. He takes his coaching duties seriously.*

*I think that Bill was more excited about the win than John. He smiled for the first time since yesterday. It was a real smile – not the awkward smile he gives me when he is trying to be brave.*

*Kelly actually came to the game. I would like to think that she was supporting her brother, but I think that she was there because she is interested in the older brother of one of the boys on John's team. She spent the game talking to him but trying not to be too obvious. It was pretty obvious to me, but the boy was probably too dumb to notice. Boys are like that. Sometimes husbands are, too. Kelly didn't say anything to me about this boy, so I guess she must like him. I thought that when she was older that we would share secrets like this. I guess she didn't want to be seen talking to the bald lady in front of her crush.*

*All in all, a pretty good day.*

# APRIL 20

We had to play again today because the first game was pushed by the rainout to yesterday. We lost 7-6. I was not allowed to pitch because I pitched yesterday. I was allowed to play third base. I was able to throw out two players at home because Doug, unlike Dan, can catch a ball.

We were winning 6-1 in the fifth inning. Then Jason started to lose interest and walked four batters in a row. When he decided to throw strikes, they were hit. Hard. By the time Coach Kraft pulled him, it was 6-5. Bob gave up two more runs. The umpire didn't help us at all, either. Dad said that there is no point worrying about the umpires because they are always right, even when they are wrong. I think that there is a "Dad Lesson" in there somewhere.

Jason also struck out with a runner on third base in the sixth inning. Dad says he has talent and a complete lack of interest in using any of it. Jason looked like he wanted to be anywhere else but standing at the plate as the winning run. I think he is one of our best players, but he doesn't try. I wish he cared more about baseball and less about girls.

# APRIL *20*

*Another day, another game. John's team lost a close game today. I'm just happy to have two hours away from being "Cancer Victim" to just think about baseball. John had a good game, but his friend, Jason, did not. He was really bad by the end. I noticed that he spent a lot of time after the game talking to girls. I guess his father's genes have already taken hold of him.*

*After the game, I tried to talk to Bill about the next few weeks, months… whenever. He didn't want to discuss it. He said that I should think about getting better. Am I the only person who knows that I'm dying? Is everybody living in a fantasy world?*

# APRIL 21

I am still mad about the game yesterday. I asked Jason why he struck out on such a bad pitch to end the game. He said that he was looking at Mary instead of the ball. Who does that? Stupid.

I told Mom what Jason said, and she laughed. It wasn't funny. Then she said, "You'll understand some day." I hate when people tell me I will understand something "someday." It's like teachers who think that they are so smart because they have the book with the answers in the back.

# *APRIL 21*

*John told me Jason struck out yesterday because he was looking at a girl. I laughed and said that he might do the same thing someday. He seemed mad. He is so different from Kelly. She was born wanting to be 18. Or 30. John has always been happy at whatever age he is at the moment. I am sorry that he is going to grow up without me.*

# APRIL 22

We lost 10-5. I pitched three innings. I gave up three runs, so I wasn't great, but Dad says that I have the best ERA on the team. I guess being the best pitcher on a bad team has some advantages. I also threw out two runners at the plate. I hit a double. I also struck out by swinging at a high pitch. Dad asked me after the game if I forgot to bring my ladder. He said that I will have to live with the shame of that pitch for many years. I don't think he was joking.

Jason almost tried to catch a foul ball. Dad said that he was impressed with his effort. I don't think he meant it. Mom wasn't at the game. Maybe she knew that we were going to lose. She has never missed one of my games before.

# *APRIL 22*

*Dr. Jacobs gave me more bad news. He told me that my test results are "disappointing." I almost apologized for not trying harder to get better. I really don't know where they learn to speak like that. Even lawyers are more direct.*

*I can't imagine a lawyer telling a death row inmate that his case was "disappointing" as they stuck the needle in his arm.*

*Bill asked the doctor if there was any other treatment that "we" (!!!) could try. He said that there were no other options, but he did mention hospice care.*

*"That's for people who are dying, not her."*

*Bill left the office and waited in the car. Dr. Jacobs told me that this was the worst part of his job. I actually felt bad for him. Of course, I felt worse for myself.*

*On the ride home, Bill held my hand. Tightly. I told him that I could handle the cancer but I didn't need a broken hand, too. He smiled and loosened his grip. A little. He acts like as long as he is touching me, I can't leave him. I wish he was right.*

# APRIL 23

After school, I stayed in town with some of my friends. We went to a store where they sell candy and ice cream. Dad calls it The Sugar Shop and thinks it is too expensive. He worries that I will get cavities and have bad teeth like him. Dad could break a tooth drinking water.

When I called home to ask for a ride, Mom told me that she would pick me up at the library. When I ended the call, a girl at the store told me that she had the same phone as me. I said, "Okay." Then I left. Later, Dad told me that the girl was probably flirting with me. I don't think she was. Maybe.

# APRIL 23

*Bill has decided to start helping me more with the housework. Before I was sick, we had very defined roles. I was in charge of the house, and Bill was responsible for the yard. There was a heated discussion early in our marriage about taking out the garbage. Bill believed that this was my job since the garbage originated inside the house. I maintained that because the garbage cans were outside, they were technically in the yard and fell within the def-*

*inition of yard work. Like most arguments, I prevailed. I told Bill that carrying out the garbage made me too tired for "anything else." It was never discussed again.*

*I wrote down laundry instructions for Bill. Then I showed him how to do laundry. I don't know how he never learned simple rules. White and red do not get washed together. Bleach is only for professionals. Bras do not go in the dryer. Ever. Bill didn't understand that rule at all. I tried to explain about underwires and how fabric can shrink but I don't think he was listening. I think that he just wanted to watch me holding a bra. What man wouldn't?*

# APRIL 24

Pink pants! I had to play my game in pink pants. Because Mom is really tired, Dad has started doing the laundry. He washed my white baseball pants with my red socks. Dad said that it was barely noticeable, and he didn't have time to buy new pants before the game. I was so embarrassed that I struck out three times. It felt like everybody was staring at me every time that I batted. I just swung at every pitch, so I could either get on base or go back to the dugout. I told Mr. Kraft that my arm was sore and asked him if I could play catcher. There was no way that I was going to stand on the mound and have everybody look at my pants. I rubbed dirt on my pants every chance I got.

We won 11-0. After the game, Coach Kraft told the team that they should all dye their pants pink. When we were walking back to the car, I saw the girl that talked about my phone yesterday. She must have seen the game. As I passed her, she said, "Nice pants. Can I borrow them?" Then she laughed and started talking to her friends. I hate Dad.

# APRIL 24

*I told John that I was very moved by his gesture of wearing pink pants to his game to support breast cancer awareness. He didn't think it was funny.*

*Bill washed John's baseball pants with red socks yesterday. He also tossed Kelly's bras in the dryer. She came in my room after she pulled her laundry out of the basket (Bill doesn't fold clothes). The bra that she was wearing had shrunk, and she looked like she was trying out for a new girl band. She doesn't have much to show, but she looked ridiculous in her mini-bra. I guess that I will be on a shopping trip with Kelly later today.*

# APRIL 25

Four bras and two pairs of "awesome" jeans later, Kelly's world has returned to normal. I wish that it was that easy for me. It was nice to go out with Kelly to do something that normal mothers and daughters do. I can't imagine Bill and Kelly shopping. Maybe I should have bought enough bras and clothes to get her through until she goes to college.

During our shopping trip, I bought two bras for myself. I don't really need them since my surgery. The replacement boobs are pretty high and solid.

After the initial shock of being told that I needed a double mastectomy, I decided that I wanted implants as soon as possible. Bill said all of the right things about loving me the way that I am and that I didn't need to have the operation for his sake. I told him that I wanted the operation for me. Having played his part as the caring husband, he agreed to go shopping with me (see the plastic surgeon).

Dr. Madison was very pleasant and empathetic. She told me that she would perform the implant surgery right after I underwent the mastectomies. She examined my breasts and took photographs to assess my frame and body type. Bill later told me that he never thought that seeing another woman feel me up would be so sickening.

I decided that I would go with C cups since I had never really liked my Ds but didn't want to drop down too far. I always felt uncomfortable with them, and I didn't like being limited in the clothes that I could wear. After we *started dating, Bill claimed that he never noticed how big I was when we first met. I didn't believe him, so I turned around and asked him the color of my eyes. He hesitated and said "green." My eyes are brown.*

*A few nights before my surgery, Bill and I had a "going away party." Life went on.*

# APRIL 25

Mom bought me new baseball pants. She also bought a lot of stuff for Kelly. I hope that Dad stops doing laundry.

## APRIL 26

*John pitched really well today. He did not finish the game because players are only allowed to throw so many pitches. Bill said it is to protect their arms. I used to pitch three full games a week in softball, but Bill said that is an underhanded motion that does not put strain on the shoulder. Still seems like baseball is for softies.*

## APRIL 26

We won 12-2 today. I almost pitched the whole game, but I hit my pitch count in the bottom of the fifth inning. Jason gave up two runs on a homerun over the center field fence. Dad said it was a great hit. I hate when he does that. He always says good things when the other team makes a great play or has a big hit. Dad just says, "Talent is talent." He's OUR coach.

# APRIL 27

*Bill surprised me today. He took the day off. He almost never does that. When Kelly was born, he stayed home with me for one day. He was so annoying that I sent him back to his office. When John came home from the hospital, he just asked if I needed anything before he went to his office.*

*We went to a local winery for lunch. The snow was gone, and the weather was warm. April in our area can be three seasons in one week – winter, spring, and summer. Bill doesn't drink because he said his mom drank more than enough for him. I had a flight of four different wines – two red and two white. On weekends, there was usually a band or singer. Since it was during the week, there were more employees than visitors and no music. At least until Bill took out his phone and just played my favorite songs. Bruce Springsteen, Jackson Brown, Barry Manilow…Yeah. I just wrote that. I liked the red wines better. Bill always knows when I need a day like this.*

# APRIL 27

In Health class today, we learned about how alcohol affects people. I don't know why they teach us about this stuff. I don't drink alcohol. I know it tastes bad because there is wine at Mass, and I don't like it. I know Kelly drank beer with her friends at a sleep over a few weeks ago. She said it made her really sick. I made $10 after she told me.

# APRIL 28

*I don't know if I need any more days like yesterday. I was so tired after we got home that I fell asleep right after dinner. Bill said I didn't use to be such a lightweight. Good thing he did not know me in college. I never did anything really stupid, but I had a good time. The statutes of limitations have run on all of the other stuff.*

# APRIL 28

I got an A on my health quiz. When I told Mom that we learned about alcohol in class, she said to not drink. I asked her when she started drinking. She said she was 30. I don't believe her. She looked like she did when I asked her about Santa Claus.

# APRIL 29

*Kelly told me that she met with her guidance counselor today. They discussed her ideas for what she wants to do after high school because she will be a junior next year. Kelly was not really prepared because she is never really prepared for anything. She told me she knows that she does not want to be a lawyer. Good. I did something right. She said she might want to be a teacher because she thinks that she could reach students like her. I was very surprised but happy to hear that she does think of the future. Even if I am not in it.*

# APRIL 29

Kelly asked me what I want to do when I am older. I was surprised because she was not yelling at me. I never really thought about it. I would like to be a baseball player, but I know a lot of kids who say that. She told me that she was thinking about being a teacher. I started to laugh, and she punched me in the chest. Hard. I would tell Mom, but she would say I was wrong to laugh at her. I would tell Dad, but he would say Kelly is mean, and I should not fight her.

# *APRIL* 30

*Today is my last birthday. I never thought that I would write those words unless Bill finally pushed me too far, and I was on Death Row. Well, I guess I am. But I put on a brave face and celebrated with the family. Nothing goes better with cancer than cake and wine.*

*Bill made his annual joke that I was born on the day Hitler killed himself. Bill is filled with useful information. Too bad none of it made us rich. It's probably better this way. I want him to find somebody who loves him for the good man that he is and his knowledge that the Treaty of Ghent ended the War of 1812 instead of somebody who wants his money, and my life insurance proceeds.*

*Kelly made the cake. It was actually good even if it was not exactly round. Or square. Not sure how something baked in a pan can come out with a different shape. John and Kelly gave me cards that I know were bought by Bill. Bill gave me a funny card with cats on it. Last year it was dogs. Next year it would have been dogs. Maybe his next woman will get penguins. Not my problem.*

*Bill bought my flowers. His present was a book about Bruce Springsteen. I hope he saved the receipt. I won't own it for long.*

# APRIL 30

Today was Mom's birthday. She is 46. That seems old, but Mom is still pretty fun. Dad said it was also the day Hitler killed himself. How does he know all these things? He does it all the time. April 15 was the day some ship sank and Abraham Lincoln died. July 2 is the day they voted to declare independence. He always wants to help me with homework. Unless it is math. Then he says to ask Mom.

Kelly made the cake. It was good but looked weird.

# MAY 1

Dad said that I stunned him today. He meant it in a good way. I pitched really well after Jason sucked. I also played an inning at catcher and threw out a runner stealing second. We won 9-7. After the game, some girls were talking to Jason. He really likes to talk to girls. I don't know why.

# *MAY 1*

*John's team won today. He played a great game as a pitcher and catcher. I really love watching him play. He can be so shy around people he doesn't know. On the field, he is a totally different person – a real leader. Sometimes Bill gets on him for not trying as hard as he can, but I think that John is just so good that it seems effortless for him. He is so different than his friend, Jason. I think that Jason is more talented than John, but he doesn't really try too hard at anything except talking to girls. I'm not sure that John could name three girls in his school.*

# MAY 2

*I realized that I didn't write about my illness or complain about anything yesterday. Good. I am trying to be more positive. Bill has tried to get me to focus on small victories like a day without pain or a day when Kelly doesn't slam a door or a day when he doesn't say something stupid. Well, one out of three isn't bad for today.*

*Kelly told me that she was angry about something one of her friends, Melissa, said today. Melissa's mother apparently didn't let her go somewhere or do something or whatever horrible things mothers do to their daughters. Melissa said that sometimes she wished her mother would just leave or die. Kelly apparently flipped out and started yelling at her about me and how she has no idea what it's like knowing your mother is sick but won't tell you anything.*

*She was still upset when she told me the story. She didn't really say much more than that, but it was nice to know that she appreciates me to some extent. It also made me feel terrible that I have brought such a harsh reality into her life. Of course, after dinner, I asked her if she had finished her homework, and she ran into her room and slammed the door so the harsh reality went back to the age-appropriate cluelessness.*

*Bill has been on the phone several times today with Coach Kraft. They are apparently worried about tomorrow's game. The team's record is 3-1 right now, and the team they are playing has a better record and "the best pitcher"*

*Bill has ever seen in this league. Apparently, this player can also hit and play any position. She must be pretty good.*

# May 2

Dad told me that tomorrow will be a "big test." He is worried about Abby Taylor. I heard that she is good from Jason, but he probably just thinks that she is good because she is cute. I'm not afraid of a girl, especially pitching.

# MAY 3

We failed the big test. Dad said that today was a "horror show." I was pulled in the third inning with the bases loaded and the score 6-1. That made me the best pitcher of the day. We lost 15-2. I struck out three times – to a girl! Abby Taylor is the only girl in the league. Dad said that he would trade me for her, but he might have to throw in Jason, and Abby Taylor's coach doesn't like his mother.

# MAY 3

*Damn. That was hard to watch. I don't know if John has ever pitched so badly. Coach Kraft pulled him in the third inning. I think that he did it as a favor to Bill. To make it worse, John struck out three times to that girl, Abby Taylor. I was sitting next to her mother the entire game. She seemed nice, if overly blonde. I almost asked her if she had used the same plastic surgeon that I did since her chest seemed as high as mine. I didn't. I did tell her that her daughter was very impressive. She thanked me and told me that Abby really loves playing but worries that boys won't like her. I told her that she didn't have to worry about my son since I don't think that he noticed girls at all. She said that someday that would change. Then she stated, "Abby certainly has noticed John. She told me several times that she was playing against him today." Interesting.*

*I would never tell John or Bill that I was glad that she did so well. I would have loved to play baseball at her age, but I was lucky that my town had softball for girls. I could have taken Abby deep.*

# MAY 4

Abby Taylor called me tonight. I asked her where she got my phone number. She said she asked Jason's girlfriend. I asked her, "Which one?" She laughed. She thanked me for striking out so many times because her grandfather was at the game. I hated hearing that, but she is a good player. Then she asked me about the team that I beat before she beat us. I told her that they only have three players who can hit, and they all chase off-speed pitches. She thanked me and said goodbye.

# MAY 4

*So it begins. John said he was called by a girl tonight. Kelly asked if it was his girlfriend, Abby Taylor. He told her to shut up and tried to punch her. I told Kelly to stop teasing him. But now I want to know. Was it Abby Taylor? Is she his girlfriend? What did they talk about? I remember being that age and calling boys and just being silly. The boys always seemed clueless why we called them. How could they be so stupid? We called them because we liked them.*

# MAY 5

I called Abby Taylor to ask her about the team we are playing tomorrow. She said that their best hitter is Nathan. He can hit any pitch thrown really hard, so I should just throw slower to him. Good scouting report.

# MAY 5

*I heard John on the phone. It was Abby Taylor. I asked if she was his girlfriend. I told him that I was too young to be a grandmother. He turned bright red, and I thought he was going to explode. Then he just went to his room and slammed the door. Not as loud as when Kelly does it, but she has more practice.*

# MAY 6

Tonight's game really sucked until we won 8-7 in extra innings. There were four errors by the team when I was pitching the last four innings. I wanted to walk off the mound after we gave up two runs on one horrible play, but Coach Kraft told me that he needed me to finish the game. There are usually six innings in a game, and I usually finish it. Dad says that I am our best pitcher because I don't try to do too much. I guess that is a good thing. We won because I struck out Nathan for the third out of the seventh inning. That was awesome. Abby Taylor was right.

Mom was at the game. She said that I pitched really well, but I need to run harder to first base. Great – another coach in the family. Other moms just say, "Nice game."

# *MAY 6*

*John is a mystery to me. He does what he wants and takes his time doing it. He was born eight days late, so I should have expected it. When he tries hard, he is the best player on the field. But he does not always try hard. He was thrown out running to first base when he would have been safe if he ran harder. I know he did not want to hear about it from me, but I am running out of time to tell him anything. I feel it. I know it.*

*I used to have energy to do everything. Make breakfast and get the children to school on time. Drive from school to court. Bow to judges I knew in law school who had a lower class rank than me. Come home and make dinner. Help with homework. Prepare for tomorrow's court appearances. Now I feel like an Amazon warrior if I take a shower before noon.*

# MAY 7

Jason started the game and pitched really well for three innings. His fan club (Stacy, Allison, Rachel, and Melissa) was really impressed. We were trailing 1-0 when I started the fourth inning. We lost 1-0 because Jason got picked off third base to end the game because he was talking to the girls instead of paying attention. I was at the plate when the game ended. I know I could have gotten a hit. I thought Dad was going to explode when Jason came back to the dugout but he just said, "You have to keep your head in the game, Jason. Nice pitching." I knew that meant I was going to hear about it for the next hour when we got home. I think that Dad blames me when Jason does something stupid because he is my friend and probably would not have been drafted by Dad except for that.

# MAY 7

*I skipped John's game tonight to go dress shopping with Kelly. He lost, so I made the right choice. To be more accurate, my debit card went dress shopping with Kelly, and I walked around the mall. She said that she wanted to pick something out for herself and that I would just make too many suggestions. She is right.*

*There was nothing I really needed. Except gelato, of course. As I ate my coffee and peanut butter delight, I passed a store with wedding dresses in the window. It suddenly hit me that I would never shop with Kelly for her wedding dress. Or baby clothes. Or mom jeans. That hurt. There is some pain that even gelato can't numb.*

*When I met up with Kelly, she was very excited. I was quiet, but my silences are never as loud as Kelly's, and she did not notice.*

# MAY 8

*Kelly looked beautiful tonight. I have seen her in dresses before, but this was a DRESS. It was red and stylish and fit her perfectly. Too perfectly, according to Bill. It was a little short but passed the "can she even sit down in that dress without exposing...test." The dance was a "semi-formal," which meant that girls wore dresses and most boys wore a tie. It was held at the school from 7:00 to 11:00. Which meant that Bill was nervous from 7:00 until she returned home.*

*She went with a friend who looked almost as nervous as Bill. She has known him since first grade. Nice boy and no criminal record that Bill could find. He wore a jacket and tie (which impressed me) and already has his driver's license (which terrified Bill). I told them they looked great together. That lead to an awkward silence, which was broken when Bill said, "You should get going. You don't want to be late since it only goes until 11:00, and it's a 12-minute drive if you obey all traffic rules."*

*When they left, Bill asked if I needed anything from the supermarket. The store is right across from the high school. I said no and told him that he did not need anything, either.*

*Kelly came home before midnight (11:53, according to Bill). She seemed happy. I asked her if they had a good time. She said that she only danced with him once and then spent most of the time with her girlfriends. Bill finally relaxed.*

# MAY 8

Kelly went to a dance tonight. She looked nice. Her date seemed nervous. Dad kept looking at him. Mom kept saying that Kelly looked beautiful. After they left, Dad looked at his watch a lot until Mom told him to stop worrying.

# MAY 9

*Mother's Day. John and Kelly made me breakfast. How did they know I wanted a banana and a peanut butter and chocolate protein bar? It was okay since we all had to get to the Philadelphia Art Museum early. There was a 5k run/walk held on Mother's Day every year to raise money to fight breast cancer. I started running the race 10 years ago with my firm because one of the partners had cancer, and we wanted to support her. Well, we did not want to be the lawyers who did not support her. After she died, I got her office. I think it is cursed. They should just lock the door, so nobody else gets sick.*

*I was too tired to run this year, so I walked with Bill and the kids. I did not know that Kelly had a surprise for me. She and 20 of her friends made bright pink Team Jen shirts and walked with us. They even had shirts for me, John and Bill. John looked embarrassed but wore it. Bill wiped away tears and thanked Kelly and the girls. I was so stunned that I did not know what to say. Then I blurted out, "F\*ck cancer!" I became the coolest mom ever. At least for today.*

*The culminating event was when thousands of survivors gathered at the top of the museum steps and then came marching down. Strong, brave women who fought and won. I so desperately want to be on the steps next year. I promise to clean up my language.*

# MAY 9

Mom cursed! I won't repeat it because she used a word that would get me grounded for a year. We went to the Art Museum and walked to raise money to fight cancer. It felt good to be doing something to help Mom. Kelly's friends were there, and we all wore these pink shirts that said Team Jen. Kelly said it was too bad that I didn't still have my pink pants.

# MAY 10

This morning, I fainted. Bill says that I collapsed, but he is always being dramatic. Either way, I ended up in the emergency room. I don't know why they call it an "emergency" room since they don't act like it's an emergency unless you have a heart attack or a gunshot wound. In my case, they should have called it the "sit and wait and stare at Bill" room. I guess that they wanted to see if I could sit in an exam room for five hours without fainting again. At least they sent three different nurses in the room to ask me when I had my last period and whether I felt safe at home. I told Nurse 3 that my last period was two weeks ago, but my family didn't feel safe for several days before it.

Because of some "irregularities" in my EKG, I was admitted for "observation." The E.R. doctor told me that he thought that I might need to undergo a stress test. I said that I am 46 and have cancer, and I would love to see what other stress they would like to add to my life. When I told him that I was a lawyer, he cancelled the test. He either admitted that it was unnecessary or didn't care if he saved an attorney.

After I was settled in my room, I asked Bill to go home and get my toothbrush and some things for my stay. It was difficult to watch him leave. I wanted to go with him, but the fainting scared me. I feel safer here.

# MAY 10

Today was really scary. When I came home from school, Dad wasn't home. Kelly said that Mom was unconscious in the hospital, but I didn't listen to her. When Dad came home, he said Mom was "not feeling well." I think it is more serious than that because "not feeling well" is what Mom says when she calls my school to say I am staying home sick. Dad left after dinner to take stuff back to Mom. Kelly told me to go to bed at 10:00. She was scared, too.

I did not go to our game tonight because Dad was so worried about Mom. Jason called to tell me that we won 5-3.

# MAY 11

*My thoughtful husband returned to my room last night without my tooth-
brush. However, he brought me many useful items that he believed I needed:*

* *My makeup bag. Does he want me to meet somebody in the hospital?
  The cardiologist is handsome, but I think that he might be gay, so I am
  not going to apply mascara just yet.*
* *Underwear. I own one thong, and he brings it to my hospital room?
  Why? It's not his birthday.*
* *Reading material. Two novels and a "Plan Your Disney Vacation"
  guidebook. Bill said that he knows that I always wanted to go to Disney, and he thought that it might inspire me during treatment. I can
  just picture Bill and the children carrying my ashes through the
  Magic Kingdom. I always wanted my picture taken with Goofy holding my urn.*
* *Mail. Bill brought me the bills that are due this month. He figured that
  since I have so much free time, I should pay them.*
* *Tampons. Maybe Bill should have asked the nurses in the emergency
  room.*

# MAY 11

Mom is still in the hospital. Dad thinks that she will be there for a "few days." I think that means he has no idea when she is coming home. I think Kelly misses Mom because she has been yelling at me and Dad more. She was really good at yelling at Mom. She did it a lot.

# MAY 12

*Dr. Jacobs wants me to stay in the hospital for "a few days" because I have a bladder infection. Why? I told him that I used to handle jury trials with bladder infections. (I think that I won those cases because I asked for so many breaks, and the jury liked getting away from the court room). He told me that I used to have an immune system, too. It's about time that he finally put me in my place. I respect him for it.*

*Since I am going to be here for the next several days, Dr. Jacobs wants me to try a new drug that may slow down the growth of the tumor in my lung. I thought that I was getting better last year, but a CT scan revealed a suspicious spot on my left lung. Bill was shocked when he found out because I never smoked (as far as he knew). He said he thought that I had as much chance of getting prostate cancer as lung cancer. I didn't know if he was joking or stupid. I have asked myself that question many times since we were married.*

# MAY 12

Dad said Mom has to stay in the hospital for a few more days. I asked him what it meant. He said more than one day and less than a month.

He thinks he is being funny. I want to know why she can't be home. She had been in the hospital before, but this seems more serious. Kelly looks worried. She hasn't yelled at me today.

# MAY 13

I went to see Mom in the hospital. She looked tired. Kelly stole Mom's pudding. Mom told us a story about how a pudding eating contest gave her father a heart attack.

We lost 16 to 7. Dad said that the game wasn't really that close, and we only scored in the last inning because their good pitchers were tired from running around the bases. Thanks, Dad. We also committed six errors. Jason was thrown out twice stealing second. Dad said that he must have felt guilty about stealing because he slowed down both times before reaching the base.

I hope Mom comes home soon. It was bad enough when she told me what to do. Kelly has started telling me when to do my homework (what a joke – I don't think she even knows where her text books are). She tells me when to go to bed and starts yelling if I don't. I think that Dad is too worried about Mom to tell her to stop it. Instead of yelling, I wish Kelly would learn to cook.

# MAY 13

*Bill brought John and Kelly to see me this afternoon. They asked me when I was coming home. I was really moved by their desire to see me until John told me that they wanted me to make dinner. Bill only knows how to make three things – hamburgers, hot dogs, and French toast. He is not bound by the clock, either. The children apparently did not enjoy breakfast for dinner two nights in a row.*

*They arrived when I was eating lunch. Kelly asked if she could eat my chocolate pudding. I wasn't very hungry, and I gave it to her. I told her that when I was a child, my sisters and I used to have pudding eating contests. We tried to eat as slowly as possible. The contest usually ended in a draw after my father yelled at us to finish eating or give him the pudding. He meant it. The man loved dessert. He also loved food in general. Dessert, salt, steak, and cigarettes were his favorite food groups. I guess that his heart attack should not have been such a shock.*

# MAY 14

Dr. Jacobs gave me his daily Doom Report. The medicines are not shrinking the tumor. On the positive side, my bladder infection is almost gone. The catheter may be removed later today. I will miss it – it really was convenient. Maybe I should have had one when I was pregnant with Kelly, so I wouldn't have taken so many breaks in court. Then again, the jury might not have appreciated the urine-filled bag hanging from the defense table.

Kelly was a challenge from the beginning. It took us two years of "trying." Sex is supposed to be fun, not a chore. Bill said that he was willing to "try" as long as necessary because of his great love for me. My hero.

When I was finally late, I told Bill that I would take the test after dinner. We ate very fast (no pudding eating contest that night). After the lines appeared, I had to read the directions twice to see if two lines meant pregnant or not pregnant. I don't know why they can't just have the word "pregnant" appear on the strip. After I decoded the mysterious lines, we started jumping up and down. He said that I should stop jumping or I might have a miscarriage. I assured him that only happened on television (I always wondered why so many pregnant characters who didn't want the baby always climbed ladders).

The pregnancy proceeded without any major issues (aside from the vomiting and exhaustion). Bill annoyed the hell out of me, but I knew it was motivated by love (and his natural ability to annoy me). The worst argument of our marriage occurred during this time. Bill bought filters for all of our fau-

*cets. Then he bought pitchers with filters, so that the water would be pure enough for me and the baby. One night, he caught me filling my glass directly from the tap. He started yelling and asked me why I was trying to poison our child. I flipped out and told him that I was tired of waiting for the water to run through the pitcher and that it would take less time to stand next to a melting glacier. I ordered him to sleep on the couch or under a bridge. He chose the couch because it was closer. We finally made up after I agreed to only drink twice-filtered water and gave up folding laundry (Bill worried about me leaning over to pick it up out of the basket). That promise lasted two weeks since Bill folded laundry about as well as a one-armed squirrel.*

*Tomorrow is Kelly's birthday. I will have to tell her the story of her origins (minus the "trying" details). I wonder if she will be interested or just act like she wishes that she was somewhere else.*

# MAY 14

I wish Mom was home. I am so tired of French toast. I don't know why Dad can't be like Jason's dad and just buy dinner at McDonald's every night. Apparently, that would violate a "Dad Rule." Dad says that divorced parents are allowed to be nice to their children because they don't see them every day. He thinks that makes sense. I don't.

# MAY 15

*Kelly actually listened to my stories about her birth. I told her that while she was being born, her father drove the nurses crazy, asking questions about all of the monitors that I was attached to. ("Is 94 normal? What does it mean? Is 95 better or worse?") I said he does the same thing with my monitors now.*

*I asked Kelly if there was anything that she wanted for her birthday. I expected her to ask for the usual things that 16-year-old girls want (a car, a boyfriend, a boyfriend with a car...) She said that she wanted me home. I don't know if she started crying before I did, but it was quite a moment. For the first time in my life, I was speechless. The daughter who used to ask me to drop her off a block from school, so her friends wouldn't see me...the girl who told me several times a day that I embarrassed her...Kelly wanted me home. Like the Grinch, Kelly's heart grew three sizes today.*

*Kelly and I talked for more than an hour before she had to leave for dinner with Bill and John. It was sad to see my little girl go, but I like the young woman who replaced her.*

*After dinner, Bill came to the hospital by himself. He asked me what Kelly and I had talked about. She seemed "different" to him. I told him about her birthday wish. He cried, too. At least he didn't try to hide it. He has never been able to hide things like that from me. Then again, he might cry a bit too much. I can understand moments like the one today causing the tears to flow, but Bill can't watch* Saving Private Ryan *without losing it. He told me that anybody who doesn't cry at the end of that movie has ice water in their veins. I hope it's double- filtered ice water, or Bill may end up on the couch again.*

# MAY 15

Kelly and Dad went to see Mom today. I didn't go because it is Kelly's birthday, and she wanted to go by herself. I feel bad saying it but I am glad that I didn't have to go. I hate that place. It smells weird.

When Kelly came home, she said that she was sorry that she yelled at me so much. She started crying and said that she was so scared about losing Mom. I never saw Kelly cry about anything that wasn't stupid, and it scared me a little. I think that Mom will get better. That's why people go to hospitals.

# MAY 16

*Kelly got her driving permit today! She was so nervous about taking the written test that she actually studied. Too bad there were no math or chemistry questions. Maybe she would have better grades if she needed to memorize the periodic table to drive.*

*I will let Bill take her out to practice driving. He taught her how to ride a bike. How hard could it be to teach her how to drive a car?*

# MAY 16

Kelly has a permit now. She kept saying that she did not like her picture. Dad said she made the lady take it five times and finally had to accept it when she was told that the place was closing, and she would have to come back and take the test again tomorrow if she did not get her permit today. Dad did not think that was true, but he told Kelly it was. Now he has to take her out to drive. That sounds scary. For Dad.

# MAY 17

Another close game today, but at least we won 11-9. Dad said that we should have crushed that team, but we made too many mistakes. He doesn't know if we are a good team that doesn't play well or if we are a bad team that overachieves. I joked that it's probably just bad coaching. Dad didn't smile. Ever since Mom went to the hospital, he doesn't smile much, so maybe it wasn't because of what I said.

# *MAY 17*

*Still here. I don't know if I am leaving the hospital any time soon. I may not ever leave. Dr. Jacobs asked me again if I had considered hospice care. I have considered it. Bill and I talked about it several weeks ago. Bill wants me to come home as soon as possible, even if it is only for a few weeks. I don't know if I want that for the children. When my mother was sick, she wanted to die in her own bed. She got her wish, and we got her bed. Bill still refers to it as the death bed. He absolutely refused to let it in our house until after I ordered a new mattress for it. I made him sleep on Mom's side of the bed because I had chosen my side of the bed the first time I spent the night with him, and I refused to switch sides.*

*When we were cleaning out Mom's house before it was sold, I had trouble going into the room where she died. The death bed occupied the center of the room, and I could not avoid thinking of the last time that I saw her. Her eyes were open, but she wasn't there anymore. Bill was home with the children, and I was alone with Mom until she was taken away. I can't stand the thought of John and Kelly seeing me dead. It would scare John and embarrass Kelly.*

*Bill really did not want to discuss the issue again. He told me that Breakfast for Dinner V was not appreciated and the children want me home. He suggested that maybe I could leave the hospital at meal times, feed them all, and Kelly could use the driving practice to bring me back here. I think that he was kidding. Then again, it is Bill.*

# *MAY 18*

*Dr. Jacobs is going to discharge me tomorrow. My infection has been cured, and there is no effective treatment for the tumor. I asked him if he was just tired of seeing me every day. He didn't answer, so I guess I am as big a pain in the ass as I thought I was. Good.*

*John came to visit me today. He wanted to hear about his birth. There were many things that I did not tell him. It took more than two years to conceive him. Probably less than two years if you count the times that I fell asleep before we could "try." Being a new mother is really effective birth control.*

*After more than a year of failure, Bill and I saw a specialist. He thought that I was probably not the source of the trouble since I had already delivered one child. Bill was not thrilled to learn that he might be the problem, but he underwent the required tests with his usual sense of humor.*

*In order to provide a sample, he had to "save up" for several days. When he finally made his deposit, he had to take a cab to the doctor's office carrying his plastic bottle in a paper bag. He said that it was embarrassing enough to deliver his fresh semen to an attractive nurse at the front desk. As he was leaving, a woman came up to the desk carrying a "mason jar filled half-way to the top." Bill claimed that he was not exaggerating, and that he wanted to tell the woman that she was obviously the one with fertility problems.*

*After Bill had surgery to "straighten some things out," we finally made John. Sometimes when he feels unappreciated, Bill shows me the scar from his operation. Well, he did until I offered to compare his three-inch incision to the scars on my chest. I won that argument.*

*I did tell John that he was a much easier pregnancy than Kelly. Kelly was even well-behaved for most of it. At first, Kelly was excited to learn that she was going to have a sibling. She didn't start disliking him until after he was old enough to touch her toys.*

*I told John that when he was born, he immediately peed on the floor. It was quite an impressive fountain. Even the doctor laughed. John loved that story.*

*I better go to sleep (not that anybody really sleeps in a hospital). I'm going home tomorrow – at least until I have to return here for the next crisis.*

# MAY 18

I visited Mom again. She told me that when I was born, I pissed on the floor. I kept laughing about it all the way home. Dad was annoyed until I told him why I was laughing. He actually smiled. I think he is also in a better mood because Mom is coming home tomorrow. Finally. No more French toast.

# MAY 19

*I was supposed to be released at 9:00 A.M., but the person assigned to kick me to the curb was delayed. I asked Bill if we could just make a break for it, but Mr. Rules said that we should wait. I was finally discharged at 11:30.*

*The ride home was very quiet. At least Bill was. I wanted to talk to him about the things that we needed to do in the next few weeks but he just said, "Hmmm. I know."*

*When we passed our church, he stopped speaking completely. We were married there, and the children were baptized there. I know that my funeral will be there. So does Bill.*

*I thought about the wedding as we continued driving. I loved my dress, especially since it was on sale and did not require many alterations. One of my friends was married that same summer and spent $5,000 on her dress. Three years later, she spent more than that on her divorce lawyer.*

*Bill looked so handsome, and I found his nervousness appealing. When my father escorted me to the front of the church, Bill just stood at the altar. Dad and I stared at him, and he stared back. Jack finally pushed him, and he came to get me. He was so nervous that he shook my hand and kissed my father on the cheek.*

*We exchanged the standard vows because I didn't trust him to write his own. Before the wedding, Bill had tried out a draft of his vows on me, which*

*I made him burn and will not repeat here. They were amusing, and we did complete 83 percent of them before I got sick.*

*After the reception, my mother helped me out of my dress. Bill came in the room while I was changing and started to leave. He then turned around and said, "Hey, we're married. I'm staying." My mother laughed, and she left us alone. Nothing happened.*

*Our honeymoon was in Bermuda. Bill had originally proposed London because he wanted to go somewhere with historical significance. I wanted to go to Hawaii, but it was too expensive, and neither of us could take that much time off from work. We finally settled on Bermuda because the residents have British accents, and there was sand. It was truly beautiful, and I regret that we never returned with Kelly and John. Then again, Kelly would brood, and John would say it was stupid, so it was probably better to not ruin the memory.*

*I wanted to make dinner but Bill said that I looked too tired. Too tired? I wasn't planning on killing a cow myself. Instead, we ordered pizza and cheesesteaks from our favorite place. I always liked the food there, but after being in the hospital, it tasted better than ever. I had the cheesesteak with everything on it and two slices of mushroom pizza (Bill says that mushroom pizza is a crime against humanity – like the designated hitter). With my luck, they will cure my cancer and then I will die from high cholesterol.*

*It will be wonderful to sleep in my own bed. Well, it will be wonderful when Bill finally finishes washing the sheets and makes the bed. I don't know how he will get by after I am gone. At least I won't have to worry about him having any women stay over in our bed if he never changes the sheets.*

# MAY 19

Mom came home today. I was really happy to see her. Even Kelly seemed happy – and that doesn't happen often anymore. We had pizza from Radnor Pizza. We ordered a half-pepperoni and half-mushroom pizza. Dad made Mom call in the order because he refused to order pizza with mushrooms on it. He also believes pizza should never have ham, chicken, pineapple, anchovies, extra cheese, peppers, or Canadian bacon on it. He says it is a crime. I agree with Mom that Dad has too many rules.

# MAY 20

*I slept until 10:30. It was great. Bill stayed home until I woke up. I told him to go to work because I know that he has been falling behind with all of the time that he has spent with me.*

*When I got out of bed, I decided to make coffee. It took me 10 minutes to find the coffee maker. I always kept it on the counter, but Bill doesn't drink coffee. He told me later that he cleaned it and put it away "where you keep it." I know that my medications have clouded my thinking in the past year, but I don't recall ever placing the coffee maker under the sink.*

*As I continued making breakfast, I found the frying pan in the cabinet above the refrigerator, knives mixed in with spoons and spoons intermingled with forks. I don't know how a man could live in the same house for more than a decade and not know where to place a spatula. Bill is the same man who organizes his ties by color and places his grilling supplies in precise order.*

*It is strange being home alone. I was used to having John and Kelly home during the week when they had days off from school. For some reason, Bill was always too busy at work to take time off. He works directly for an insurance company, so the attorneys are essentially employees who are expected to work more hours than the rest of the staff. Since he also has to bill hours, he never leaves early for holiday weekends or blizzards. He told me that the secretaries and paralegals have never felt the need to stay late. I think that his secretary has attended her mother's funeral three times in the last two years.*

*I plan on making dinner for the family. I don't think that Bill moved the microwave, but I better check before I start cooking.*

*I called my secretary this morning. She was happy to hear from me and told me that everybody in the office misses me. I asked her the status of some of my cases, but I haven't really handled many of the files for the last six months. One of the associate lawyers, Amy, has been working on most of my big cases. Well, she works on them when she isn't planning her wedding. I shouldn't complain since she is a good attorney, and I enjoyed watching the videos of the bands that she is researching for the reception. I do think her wedding dress shows too much cleavage, but I'm not going to be the one to tell her that. I'm not her mother. Then again, I won't be there when Kelly gets married, so maybe I should.*

*I would like to go to the office, but I feel like the people there have moved on with their lives. When I started at the firm, there was an old attorney who used to visit the office several times a week. He had retired a year earlier, but I think he realized that he had no life outside of his job. People used to make excuses to disappear before lunch time, so they didn't have to turn down his invitations. I used to feel sorry for him, but I am starting to understand how he feels. I don't want people to start hiding from me or making me feel like I am an annoyance. I have Kelly for that.*

*John was really down on himself after the game. Apparently, he didn't pitch well, and the team played badly. If I was coaching the team, they would run a lap around the field for every error they made. I suggested that to Bill, but he said that the team would have to run a marathon after today.*

*Speaking of meals, I have finally restored order to the kitchen. I sorted the silverware, freed the coffee cups from the drinking glass shelf, and broke up the orgy between the casual dishes and the everyday dishes. Bill wanted to know why we didn't use the casual dishes every day. I don't know, but I didn't tell him that. I explained that some days are just more casual than others. I think that satisfied him. Maybe I should have asked him to explain why men sleep on the pillows with shams on them, but women don't. Doesn't he know that the universe has rules?*

# May 20

Terrible game. We lost 9-2. I walked three batters in one inning. The team had four errors in one inning. Four. I didn't want to talk about it when Mom asked me about the game. She told me that I can only control how I pitch and not how the team fields. That made sense. Too bad she can't be a coach. I don't think she has the energy – or patience for Jason.

I saw Abby Taylor when I was leaving the field. Her game was after mine. I said, "Good luck" because they were playing a team ahead of us in the standings.

She smiled and said, "Thanks. Sorry your team sucked today. I watched you pitch. Not bad."

# MAY 21

Abby Taylor came up to me in school today. She told me that she won her game. I asked her to beat some more teams. She smiled. She has a nice smile. Maybe I shouldn't have teased her about her braces last year.

# *MAY 21*

*I felt too tired to get out of bed this morning. Bill took Kelly out to practice driving. He said she did "okay" but also said, "That's why cars have bumpers." Kelly said nothing. Sometimes, Kelly's silence is louder than anything she says. They will try again "soon."*

*Bill found the shopping list that I prepared yesterday and went to the supermarket for me. He didn't tell me that he was going because he knew that I would have tried to stop him.*

*Bill didn't do too badly. He managed to buy most of the items on the list. He bought tuna (10 cans because they were on sale), cereal (four boxes of Frosted Flakes, also on sale), and milk. He purchased some extra items because he wanted to surprise me. How did he know that I wanted shrimp and a party tray of cheese, pepperoni, and crackers? He even bought more tampons. A man willing to do that is truly worth keeping. I didn't need them, so I told Bill to give them to Kelly. I don't know if she will ever speak to me again.*

# MAY 22

This morning, Bill told me to take a shower and eat breakfast because we had to go "somewhere." I was worried that he was going to drive me out in the country and kick me out of the car after I tricked him into giving Kelly tampons. When we crossed the Walt Whitman Bridge, I figured that he was just going to dump my body in Camden.

After we got on the Atlantic City Expressway, I was excited. Bill said that he thought that I needed to get out of the house, and the casinos missed my donations. I never won or lost a lot of money, but I really enjoyed gambling. We first started going to Atlantic City the summer after our first year of law school (the trip when Dot essentially called me a whore). I always played video poker and video black jack. We won $50 that first trip, which covered the cost of our stay at Dot's Pleasure Palace. Winning the first time that you go to a casino is bad because it makes you come back.

We used to go to the casinos after spending the day at Ocean City. We didn't have enough money to rent a room, so we would get up early on Saturday morning and drive to the beach. By 3:00, we were ready to gamble. Bill would change out of his suit in a bathroom on the boardwalk. I often changed in the car while Bill drove. I wonder if my children know that their mother could put on a bra at 50 miles per hour without flashing the oncoming traffic?

After Bill parked the car, we went to my favorite casino. They are all pretty much the same, but I won more than I lost there, so that was our des-

*tination. We found the quarter machines and each inserted $20. Bill bet five quarters at a time, and I bet three. This always drove Bill crazy. When he won, he would win more, but I was able to play longer. Today, Bill won $30, and I won $25 before lunch, so we felt like high rollers.*

*For lunch, we ate at a buffet in the casino. The food wasn't terrible, but the expectations are lower when you drop below $12 for "all you can eat." Considering how many people interpreted "all you can eat" literally, I was worried that they would run out of food before we got to the cashier.*

*When we returned to the floor, we decided to try the slot machines. After dropping $10, we moved to another machine. It was very exciting when three sevens appeared. Because Bill bet five quarters instead of three, we won $500. Three ancient women who smelled like smoke and cheap perfume crowded around us and said that we were very lucky. Bill said that the luckiest day of his life was the day that he met me, but he didn't mind the money. The women laughed and seemed to fall in love with him. Bill has that ability. Of course, he thinks that waitresses love him, too, but they really just want bigger tips.*

*After our big win, we decided to go home. I thanked Bill for a wonderful date. He said that he was free whenever I wanted to go out – unless the old ladies called him first. I laughed. He didn't. I had told Bill months ago that I expected him to date after I was gone, but now I am worried that his new girl-friend may be on Social Security. That's fine. She will probably dump him after she sees his reckless gambling at the quarter slots.*

# MAY 22

Mom and Dad went gambling in Atlantic City today. Mom really likes to do that. I guess it's fun if you win. They were gone until almost 8:00. Kelly was supposed to be in charge of me, which means that I was on my own. At least Radnor Pizza is in walking distance.

# MAY 23

*My big day out really drained me. I slept late today. Bill told me that he had to be in court by 9:00, so he let me sleep and did not wake me up when he left. He left me a note on his pillow that said he loved our date and that he called the old ladies to break up with them.*

*While eating breakfast, I started reading the newspaper. I started with the obituaries, just to make sure that I hadn't died yesterday. Lately, I have been fascinated by obituaries because I know that mine will be written sooner rather than later.*

*There were several interesting notices:*

* *Josephine Murphy, 99. Josephine was a quitter. Why struggle to get to 99 years old and then die before the 100-year finish line? I also thought that it was ridiculous that her picture was at least 60 years old. Since people who knew her must know that she didn't look like she was 39 when she died, why pretend that she never got older? When I told Bill about this, he promised to use my high school graduation picture for my obituary. Great. I want my perm to be immortalized.*
* *Ella Hurvitz, 17. My first thought was that this was such a tragedy, and she was so pretty. Why do people always notice whether a dead young person was pretty or handsome? I can't imagine saying, "Well, she was kind of fat and had bad skin, so I guess it isn't too sad." Ella*

*was a senior at Kelly's school. She had been fighting a brain tumor for three years. Maybe I will see her soon.*

\*    *Mike Jones, 33. Mike "died suddenly." I always hate when people "die suddenly." I want to know the details. Heart attack? Suicide? Car accident? Wolves? Sometimes you can get a clue from the end of the obituary, where donations are suggested. "In lieu of flowers, donations can be made to the Ellen Jones legal defense fund."*

*Bill and I have not really discussed the arrangements for my funeral. We both have Wills, and Bill essentially gets everything. I don't know where I will be buried. Bill suggested sprinkling my ashes over the casino.*

# MAY 23

My Social Studies teacher said that we had to find a story in a newspaper and give a summary of it to the class. I asked Mom if we had a newspaper. She said that it was in the kitchen. It was open to a page with names and pictures of dead people. I don't know why anybody would read that. It's sad. And creepy.

We won 6-1. I did not do anything special.

# MAY 24

*I started working on my own obituary. I don't want it to be boring, but I don't want it to be too quirky. My serious draft:*

*Jennifer (nee Reilly) Fitzgerald, 46.*

*Jen lost her battle with breast cancer after a long illness, but she never lost her spirit. She is survived by her loving husband, Bill, and impressive children, John and Kelly. Jen was a loving mother, aunt, and friend. She was also a partner at the firm of Weiss and Murphy, where she was respected (but not loved) by associates and adversaries as well. She was the best member of the firm's softball team and organized great Christmas parties. In lieu of flowers, donations may be made to the charity of one's choice.*

*What I want to say:*

*Jennifer Fitzgerald, 46.*

*Jen was angry to die on _____ after a long (but not long enough) battle with breast cancer. She is survived by her awesome husband, Bill, quiet son, John, and moody but mostly loving daughter, Kelly. Jen did not have any hobbies and did not belong to any groups, although she did have a glass of red wine every Thursday night. In addition to tending to her family, Jen billed enough hours and kissed enough ass to become a partner at her law firm – several years later than she deserved. Jen was a good friend to her emotionally needy friends who never realized that married men were not going to leave their wives, more than one glass of red wine on Thursday was a problem, and they did look fat in that dress. In lieu of flowers, Jen would like her family and friends to make dinner reservations at their favorite restaurant and be happy that they are not dead.*

# MAY 24

Mom asked me if I had any funny stories about her. She said she was writing something. I said it was funny when she cursed in front of Kelly and her friends at the museum.

# MAY 25

*Bill thinks that I should use the second obituary. He even suggested a few things to include. They will be burned like his proposed wedding vows. Whenever I ask him where he gets his thoughts, he always says, "You should hear the things I don't say out loud." He is an odd, loving man. I am lucky. Well, except for the terminal illness.*

# MAY 25

Abby Taylor looked unhappy today. She told me that she did not feel good. She said something about cramps. I have had that, too, if I don't drink enough water or run too long.

# MAY 26

I am jealous that Mom gets to stay home all day. She always makes me go to school no matter how sick I am. I wish that I could watch TV and take naps this week.

# MAY 26

*I am starting to go crazy at home. I don't know how people can stay home and watch TV all day. I have seen more cheating lesbians, secret hookers, and "you're not the father" revelations to last a lifetime – and that was just one show. I also can't believe what the parties get away with on the judge programs. I stopped counting objections and hearsay statements after the first 10 minutes. The lawyer commercials are also entertaining, especially since I have beaten every one of the attorneys who "promise to fight the insurance companies and get you justice."*

*Some of the ads did make me wonder about my career choice. If I wasn't sick, maybe I could become a truck driver. I might also work in the exciting field of computers, or as a medical records clerk, or paralegal (just what the professions needs – more bad paralegals). I'm not sure if I have the strength to be an auto technician. Of course, I could just spend my time investing in gold, silver, or real estate without putting any money down. Who knew that there were so many career paths to wealth if I just called the right number TODAY?*

# MAY 27

Mom went to see her doctor today. She and Dad were pretty quiet tonight. I don't know if that is good or bad. Kelly keeps saying that Mom is going to die. I don't believe that because I don't believe most of the things that Kelly says. She knew the truth about Santa Claus years before I did, and she lied to me every time I asked about him.

# MAY 27

*Bill and I visited Dr. Jacobs this morning. There were no new treatments to discuss, and the test results were uniformly bad. It must be serious since Bill didn't make any stupid jokes.*

*I felt weak during the exam, which consisted of listening to my lungs. Dr. Jacobs asked me again about hospice, and I again refused. I do not want John and Kelly living in the place where I die. That would be too hard on them. I told Dr. Jacobs that when I can't be taken care of at home, I will go to the hospital and relax with good drugs. It's funny that I never even tried pot, and now I have a doctor promising me morphine. John and Kelly will be so surprised to learn that I am such a badass.*

*On the way home, Bill was quiet in his usual post-Dr. Jacobs way. As we drove past our church, he suddenly shouted, "Yellow car!"*

*I started laughing. When we would go on long trips (which was more than 10 minutes to my children), we played a game where the first person to see a yellow car would shout, "Yellow car!" and get a point. Whomever had the most points at the end of the trip won the game. Eventually, we added "pink car." It took more than a month, but Bill almost got into an accident when he stopped suddenly and pointed down a side street to a pink car. He talked about it way too long.*

# MAY 28

Mom is always tired, but today she seemed really out of it. Mom was in bed when I got home. She and Dad stopped talking when I came in the room. I hate when they do that. It makes me wonder what I'm missing. I can't ask Kelly because she keeps telling me that Mom is dying. There is no way that I am going to believe that. Moms don't die before their children.

# *MAY 28*

*Memorial Day weekend. I guess it would be more exciting if I was actually working. A holiday when you aren't working is just another day. It will be good to have Bill, John, and Kelly home for three days. Well, maybe one day. Kelly and John usually are ready for a knife fight if they are together more than 24 hours.*

*Once again, Bill surprised me. He told me at breakfast that he had rented a house for the weekend in Ocean City. Since the children have a half-day of school (lazy teachers!), we could leave by 1:00. To be honest, I felt exhausted when I woke up this morning, but I felt invigorated when he told me. Where was this impulsive man for the last few years? He refused to go to Disney World a few years ago because he thought it was too different from our usual vacations. He is the only man I know who would go to England for the food. Now that I am sick, he is Adventure Bill. Well, to the extent that Ocean City is an adventure.*

*The children were happy when they came home from school. Well, Kelly didn't complain, so I viewed that as happy. They packed quickly. I didn't pack much, either, since we were only going away for three days. On the other hand, Bill filled our suitcase with clothes for all conceivable weather conditions from a blizzard to a hurricane. When I asked him why he needed two pairs of jeans and two pairs of shorts, he told me that he needed "backup clothes" in case it rained. He also had a backup sweatshirt, backup sneakers, and three polo shirts. He decided to be risky and only brought one jacket.*

*The traffic wasn't "too bad." This is code in Philadelphia for "I could have walked there faster." When we crossed the 9th Street bridge from Somers Point, Bill told everybody to be quiet and turned off the radio. He loves to listen to the sound as we drove over the metal grates where the sections of the drawbridge meet. He always says that it sounds like summer to him. I agree.*

*Bill rented a three-bedroom unit on the top of a house on 16th Street. It was beautiful and decorated very nicely. There was a balcony that overlooked the boardwalk and the beach. I told Bill that he had done very well in his selection. Bill just smiled and said, "Dot died. I needed to find a new place."*

*While Bill and I sat on the balcony, John and Kelly went to the beach. As I watched them run to the ocean, I thought back to when they were small and didn't want to kill each other. Kelly would spend hours playing with John, and they built sand castles together. Well, she built them, and he pretended to be a monster and kicked them. Now, they separated at the water's edge. John started playing football with some boys that he knew from school. Kelly swam in front of the lifeguards, stood up and posed, swam again and posed again. I admired her confidence. Bill was ready to storm the beach if any lifeguard spoke to her. I will not miss those looming battles.*

*After they came back from the beach, John and Kelly wanted to go to the boardwalk. Bill reminded them to take their phones and where to find bathrooms. I gave up trying to figure Bill's thoughts many years ago. Properly in-*

structed and financed by Bill's generous wallet, they left the house and headed towards the stores and rides. I knew that John was meeting two boys from school. Kelly said that her friend, Sarah, was going to meet her at the Music Pier at 9th Street. I was sure that Sarah's older brother, Adam, would be there, but Bill didn't know that. I almost told him a few minutes later, just to see if he would run to 9th Street, but I didn't want him to have a heart attack. He was my date for the evening.

When we left for dinner, it was 85 degrees and sunny. Bill bravely decided not to take his jacket. I was going to joke with him about it, but that would have made him take it. Bill drove to a restaurant in the next town over that was on the bay. I decided to order red wine, and Bill asked me if that was a good idea with my medicines. I told him that if I lived long enough to become an alcoholic that I would start going to AA meetings. I knew that I shouldn't say things like that, but I am tired of just being a cancer patient and watching my words. Bill let it go.

It was so nice to just sit and talk. Bill must have thought so as well because he only checked his phone eight times, "just to make sure" that Kelly or John didn't call.

When we returned to the house, John and Kelly were back. They must have been tired because they weren't arguing. Quite a day.

# MAY 28

When I came home from school, Mom told me to pack for a trip to the beach. Dad rented a house in Ocean City for the weekend. I asked her if Kelly was coming, too. Unfortunately, she was. She probably just wants to talk to lifeguards. I bet they can't wait to talk to her – if they like moody, scary girls with flat chests. I think Abby Taylor looks better than Kelly, but I have never seen her in a bathing suit.

Mom and Dad wanted to go to dinner at some boring place with expensive fish. Kelly and I walked on the boardwalk down to 9th Street where people hang out. Kelly disappeared, but I didn't miss her. I thought that Jason and Brad from school would be there, but I didn't see them. I did see Abby Taylor. I didn't know her parents had a beach house. She was with some girls and boys, and they all were telling stupid jokes and screaming a lot. I hung out with them because I didn't know anybody else. Abby Taylor acted like a girl with the other girls (so much giggling and shrieking). It was weird to see her with other girls since I usually only see her with boys in baseball uniforms. She looked good – definitely better than Kelly.

# MAY 29

*I woke up at 6:00 A.M. When I opened my eyes, Bill was looking at me. It scared me at first because I wondered if I did something wrong to wake him up. He just kissed me and said that he didn't want me to sleep through breakfast. We ate French toast and sausages on the balcony. I turned to watch the sunrise over the ocean. When I looked back at Bill, I could see that there were tears in his eyes. I joked that the sausage was a little overcooked, but that it was no reason to cry. He said that he could not believe that a world with such beauty could be so cruel to us. I squeezed his hand and said that we were lucky to have found each other, and I wouldn't have wanted a longer life with anybody else. I meant it.*

*I was tired by the time John and Kelly woke up, so I rested in bed. Bill told me that he was going to rent a boat and take them fishing. I have been on a boat with Captain Bill on two occasions, and I did not want to go on a third. For a man of such caution on land, he is a wild man on the water. I wished John and Kelly luck and settled in with a book.*

*The sailors returned at 4:00, sunburned and smelling like several awful things. Bill was covered in mud and soaking wet. Apparently, he fell out of the boat. Twice. After he showered, he stated loudly that it was a good thing that he had his backup shorts and backup sneakers. Kelly and John kept looking at each other and laughing, so I was sure that there were details about the voyage that would never be revealed. It was nice to see.*

*The children wanted to go to the boardwalk again, so Bill repeated the phone and bathroom instructions and sent them out. He asked me if I wanted to go, too. I said that I wouldn't feel up to walking that far. Once again, he surprised me. He had borrowed a wheelchair from a friend who runs a physical therapy center and hidden it under chairs in the car. For a moment, I was embarrassed at the thought of being pushed on the boardwalk like an old woman. Bill told me that dinner was Salvatore's Pizza and Polish water ice. I blurted out, "Wheel me, Stud," and off we went.*

*The roll up the boardwalk was actually romantic. The moon was rising over the ocean as we neared Salvatore's. I was surprised at the ease that Bill pushed me as he wasn't exactly strong. Or fit. When we met, he weighed 175 pounds. Two children later, he weighed 200. I teased him once by asking him when he was going to lose the baby weight. He was not amused. At least he still had his hair. I wish that I had mine.*

*The pizza was awesome. I ate it sitting by the railing, looking out at the beach. I often wondered if the pizza tasted so good because I associated it with the beach and good times with Bill. Maybe if it came from a shop near my house, it wouldn't be nearly as good. The Polish water ice was also great.*

*Bill pushed me to the end of the boardwalk and then started back. As we passed the 9th Street Music pier, we saw Kelly and John in a crowd of teenagers. Kelly was talking to boys. John was talking to boys. The girls who looked to be John's age were probably talking to each other about the boys who were not talking to them. I could feel Bill start to steer me towards the swirling youth mob. I warned him to stay away. They were just hanging out, and I wanted Kelly and John to enjoy their night. They would be sad soon enough.*

*When we returned to the house, Bill helped me up the steps. He was strong enough, even though he did have thin arms. I once pointed that out, too. It was also not appreciated. Bill said that he was more than willing to provide me with a list of my flaws, but he didn't see the point. He was right. By the time that we got upstairs, I was tired and said that I needed to go to bed. I could tell that Bill was concerned about me since that kind of line usually made him say something stupid and inappropriate (unless it was Saturday night, in which case it was stupid but not inappropriate).*

# May 29

Dad took me and Kelly on a boat today. Kelly wanted to go fishing, so we rented poles and bought bait. I don't think that Kelly's friends would believe that she likes to fish. I know she likes it more than me. Fish stink – even more than Kelly.

Dad let me and Kelly take turns driving the boat. I'm glad that he did because when Dad steers, it is very scary. I guess he doesn't have any rules when he is on the water.

Later, we went back to the boardwalk. It was pretty much like last night, except that Brad and Jason were there. Abby Taylor was there, too, but I didn't talk to her as much. I don't think that she really cared because her screaming friends were there.

# MAY 30

*Last night's stroll/roll wiped me out. I slept until 10:00. We decided to come home today instead of Monday to have a day to rest before everything started up again on Tuesday. I think Bill just wanted to avoid traffic. Or he had enough worrying about Kelly talking to boys at the beach.*

*By the time that I woke up, Bill and the children had cleaned the house and packed their suitcases. I asked Bill if he was sure that he felt comfortable having both pairs of backup jeans zipped away in the suitcase. He just smiled and brought me breakfast. I think that one of the saddest things about being sick is that Bill is too nice to me. It makes me feel too different. Cranky Bill is more fun.*

*When we drove home, the traffic was light. Most people who own a house at the beach stay as late as possible before heading home. I worked with a lawyer who would leave his beach house at 5:00 A.M. to be at work on Mondays by 7:30 A.M. Considering that his wife left him for another lawyer who used to stay at his beach house until 8:30 A.M., beating the traffic may have come at a steep price. He told me once that he missed his beach house more than his ex-wife. Maybe Bill's soft stomach and scarecrow arms weren't so bad after all.*

*After dinner, I thanked Bill for the trip. John and Kelly mumbled something which might have been appreciative in nature, so Bill accepted it as thanks.*

# May 30

I thanked Dad for the trip. I think that Kelly thanked him, too, but she was so quiet that Dad said only dogs could hear her. I think that Mom really enjoyed the trip. I hope that this helps her get better.

# MAY 31

*It is good to be home. And do laundry. Not sure how three days away can generate so much, even though Bill usually only wears about 10 percent of what he packs. I will go to bed early tonight because I have another visit to Dr. Doom tomorrow.*

# MAY 31

Mom washed clothes today. No pink pants. It was fun to go to the beach. Things are back to normal. We won our final regular season game 4-2. I had two hits. Dad said the second hit was an error. Why does he do that?

# JUNE 1

*Dr. Doom lived up to his name. The tumor in my lung is growing, All of my test results suck. He told Bill that the beach trip was probably too much for me. Bill told Dr. Jacobs... Well, he didn't agree with his assessment of our travel plans. Dr. Jacobs told me that he can make me comfortable and treat infections, but a cure is "unlikely at this stage." I know that he is right, but I don't know how to tell the children.*

*I intended to tell the children how bad things are today. I really did. Before they came home from school, my office manager called and told me that our firm had four tickets available for tonight's Phillies game. I accepted them gladly. I will be dying all week. I can talk to them tomorrow.*

*The game is against the Chicago Cubs. Bill hates the Cubs. How a man can hate a team known as the "Lovable Losers" is difficult to understand unless you know Bill. In college, "The First Guy" was a Cubs' fan. Even though the guy turned out to be nothing special and was actually a jerk, Bill has hated the Cubs since we exchanged "history stories" after our first date. Then again, Bill hates every team, and I certainly didn't hook up with that many men. Other than the Unlovable Loser, I stayed in the National League East.*

*Tonight should be a nice night out for the children.*

# JUNE 1

Tonight was scary. Really scary. Maybe Kelly is right. I don't want to write about it.

# June 2

Bill always tells John that he shouldn't bet on sports. After last night, I know that I should not predict "nice nights out for the children."

We arrived an hour before the game, so we could park closer to the stadium ("Ballpark," I can imagine Bill yelling as I write this). Walking for more than 15 minutes at a time is becoming a problem, and I didn't want another wheelchair ride. We took our time getting to the entrance gate. Well, Bill and I did. Kelly and John took their tickets and raced ahead. Since we were all going to end up in the same seats anyway, it was not a big deal to me. Bill said it would be nice if they could walk with their mother. I said that it would be sad if they wanted to be seen with their parents at their age.

When we got to our seats, Bill said that he would buy me dinner and that I had a choice of hot dogs or chicken fingers and French fries. I told Bill that I would have the chicken since I didn't know if the hot dog was a healthy choice. He gave me an odd look until he realized that I was joking.

In addition to my food, Bill brought me a beer. I thanked him and said that I couldn't make any promises for that night. He laughed and said he was not trying to get me drunk. He just wanted me enjoy the full baseball experience. I was worried that I was going to end up with peanuts, popcorn, crackerjack, and a foam "Phillies #1 Phan" finger. I was wrong. They were out of peanuts.

By the seventh inning, the Phillies were up 8-1 on the "Daves," as Bill called them. The First Guy was named Dave. A lot of fans were starting to *leave, but I knew that I would be there until the final out of the ninth inning. One of Bill's rules is that you can never leave a game until it is over. Ever. He is so different from my father. My dad never stayed to the end of games because he wanted to "beat the traffic." I think that I was in college before I realized that the eighth inning was not an extra inning.*

*I don't know what happened after the seventh inning because I passed out during "Take me out to the ball game." I woke up in Thomas Jefferson University Hospital several hours later. Bill told me that he was no longer buying me beer, as I was clearly a light-weight. I didn't laugh because this event scared me.*

*John and Kelly waited at the hospital until I was awake. I told them that I was feeling better, and I don't think that they believed me. They went home with Bill because I had to undergo tests. Bill told me that he would bring me a bag of things from home in the morning. He promised that he would not pack tampons.*

# JUNE 2

Mom is in the hospital again. She has been there since we went to the Phillies game. I don't know why she keeps going there, but it can't be good. I wish that I could talk to Dad about what is going on, but he gets angry if I ask questions. Maybe he is scared, too.

# JUNE 3

*Dr. Jacobs was very quiet when he visited me in the hospital this morning. He told me that I had pneumonia. He said that I was clearly exhausted, and that he thought that my beach trip and Phillies game were too much activity. I asked him if I should have had wine instead of beer. For the first time, I saw Dr. Jacobs get angry.*

*"Is everything a joke to you? Do you want to die in a parking lot?" he snapped.*

*I probably should have been quiet, but I am running out of time to say anything. I went back at him, "Does it matter where I die? I don't have much time left, and I'm going to run it out until the end. I'm sorry that you couldn't cure me, but don't tell me how to live – or die."*

*He left without saying anything else.*

*When Bill arrived, I was still fuming. Bill was impressed with the "run it out" baseball reference. He suggested that it might not be a good idea to piss off my doctor. I told him that it didn't really make a difference. I was stunned when he agreed with me. For the first time he seemed beaten. He said that he wanted me to be happy and that he wasn't looking for miracles anymore. I told him that I wasn't looking for anything because I had found everything already when I met him. For the first time in many years, too many years, Bill had nothing to say.*

# June 3

Dad was at the hospital all day. I don't know what he and Mom talk about. It must be pretty boring. I really wanted to talk to him about what is going on with Mom when he got home, but he was acting really weird. He was very quiet – and he is almost never quiet. He looked like he does when our team loses a game.

# JUNE 4

*Tests. Tests. More Tests. Almost all of the results were bad. I think that the only thing that I have going in my favor is low cholesterol, and I don't have prostate cancer. Dr. Jacobs came to see me before lunch. He didn't discuss the tests. He sat down beside my bed, held my hand, and told me that he needed to speak to me not as a doctor but as a friend. I said that I was flattered but that I just didn't think that it was the right time to leave Bill. He assured me that he would somehow survive my rejection. He also said that he would not be able to revive his Jewish mother if he brought home Jennifer Reilly Fitzgerald.*

*Dr. Jacobs wanted me to know that he regretted yelling at me yesterday. He also wanted to apologize for not curing me.*

*"I really thought that we" (we!?!) "would beat this. You fought harder than any patient I ever had."*

*Once he placed my battle in the past tense, I knew that the days are running out. I thanked him for everything and gave him the name of a Jewish lawyer at my firm who might pass his mother's initial review.*

*Bill was happy that Dr. Jacobs and I had made up.*

*"I was worried about you two. You seemed so perfect for each other as doctor and patient," he joked. We laughed together, probably more than we should have. I made Bill promise that he would never tell Dr. Jacobs that I had sought a second opinion after my initial diagnosis. I didn't want to hurt him.*

# JUNE 4

Dad said that we must go see Mom tomorrow. Must? That didn't sound good.

# JUNE 5

*I was cold all day. I have developed a fever, and the pneumonia is not going away. Bill told me that he brought Kelly and John to see me, but he first had to have a serious discussion with me before they came up to my room.*

*I was concerned that Bill might actually be serious until I remembered that he was already serious yesterday. The man has a limited capacity. He told me that he could not let me go until we resolved our most serious bedroom issue. I said that I didn't want to talk about "that" again. He said that it wasn't "that." It was the pillow issue.*

*Early in our marriage, Bill and I argued over his sleeping on the pillow that was covered in a sham. I told him that those pillow shams were decorative and not to be used. He replied that they were on the bed and therefore eligible for sleeping. We never really resolved the issue. Sometimes he used to switch my pillow with the sham or, even worse, his pillow. I always caught him. We finally agreed that we could each do what we wanted on our side of the bed, but we should never speak of it again. Today, I released Bill from his vow.*

*"Good. I've been sleeping on all of your pillows since you were admitted to the hospital," he confessed. If I get out of here, there will be hell to pay when I get home.*

*Having admitted violating my pillows, Bill returned with John and Kelly. I loved seeing them, but I hated them seeing me like this. John brought me a foam finger that he bought at the Phillies game. Kelly asked me if there was anything that I needed that Dad didn't bring me. I almost asked Kelly for tampons just to freak her out, but I held back. I was excited about the finger and let Kelly know that Dad was doing a great job. They stayed for about an hour, and we talked about a lot of different things. John talked about his baseball team and said he was excited about the playoffs (and that pitcher named Abby). Kelly mostly looked at me. It was the best time that I ever had in a hospital.*

# JUNE 5

I got to see Mom today. I brought her the foam "Phillies #1 Phan" finger that I bought at the game. I thought that it would look good in her room. Mom is a really big fan.

Mom asked me how baseball is going. I told her that my first playoff game is coming up. I told her that I was happy that we didn't have to face Abby Taylor's team unless we play in the championship game. Mom teased me about Abby, but I told her that she is just another player. I don't think that she believed me. Mom is pretty smart sometimes.

# JUNE 6

*Tests suck... Got that out of the way. Bill had to handle four mediations at work today, so he couldn't visit until after lunch. I told him that he needs to work as much as possible while he can. Besides, he stares at me too much and feels for my pulse every time I close my eyes. I did have company, though. My Work Husband, Ted, came to visit.*

*Ted had recruited me to come to the firm. We had been opposing counsel in a case, and he was a very good attorney. I was better. After the trial, he invited me to lunch. I usually would have said no to a request from a handsome man since I was married, but Bill had said something stupid that morning (I don't remember what), and two-year-old Kelly had thrown up on my trial bag as I was walking out the door, so I said yes.*

*At lunch, Ted told me that his firm was looking to add an experienced litigator, and some of the partners had watched the trial. They wanted to meet me and discuss joining their firm. Since I hated my boss (still do – she is not invited to my funeral since she would probably enjoy it), I agreed to work for them. Thirteen years later, I am still there. Well, to the extent that I am employed anywhere.*

*Ted and I used to have lunch together in the lunch room or, rarely, at a restaurant. Bill wasn't jealous because he first thought that Ted was gay since he wore eyeglasses with small frames. After Ted got married and bought larger frames, Bill was a little concerned. I told him that he was being stupid since*

*Ted didn't see me "that way." Bill replied that since I had breasts and a face, every male lawyer and judge in the city "looked" at me. I didn't believe it. I didn't want to believe it. Noooooooo!*

*Bill was the one who started calling Ted my "Work Husband" when I started complaining about something Ted said at work. Since Bill thought that I only complained about him, he realized that Ted played the same role in my office that Bill did in my house. He actually felt bad for Ted since he didn't get to sleep with me but had to put up with everything else that I did and said.*

*Ted looked very uncomfortable sitting by my hospital bed. He told me that the people in the office missed me and that they wanted me to get well soon. I could tell that he knew that it was a stupid thing to say, so I told him that it was. He actually seemed relieved. Ted thanked me for being such a good friend to him and his wife. He joked that since my billable hours were so bad over the past few months, I was probably getting a poor review at the end of the year. I asked him to tape it to my tombstone. We laughed. Ted bent down to kiss me when he left. Definitely not gay.*

# JUNE 6

Dad told me that he is going to be spending more time with Mom and that he was not going to work for the next few days. This is really bad. Even though Dad doesn't like his job very much, he hates to miss work. Mom always gets mad at him for checking his e-mail and voice-mail when we go away. Dad said I should try to focus on baseball and school for the next few weeks. What else would I do? I'm 12.

# JUNE 7

*Bill told me that he let his boss know that he was not going to come back to work for "a while." His boss apparently asked when that would be, and Bill told him that he would be back a week after my obituary was in the newspaper. Bill does have a way with words.*

*I'm still cold, and I am coughing more now. At night, I have an oxygen mask that helps me breathe easier. I don't like to wear it when Bill or the children visit me since it scares them. John did ask me once to put it on because he wanted to see if it would make me sound like Darth Vader. It didn't.*

# JUNE 7

We won our first playoff game 7-3. I did not pitch today because Coach Kraft wanted to save me for the next game if we won this game. Dad said that he disagreed because if we did not win today, there would not be a next game. We got lucky when we had a triple play – Coach Kraft said that he has never seen a triple play in 20 years of coaching. I was responsible for the third out when I tagged a runner coming home. Dad talked about it on the way home. And when I was doing my homework – I hate math. And after I was in bed. He opened my door and said, "That was some play."

# JUNE 8

Kelly and John surprised me this afternoon. They rode the train into the city. I made sure that they had told Bill before they left, or he would have called the police, the State Police, four hospital emergency rooms, and the FBI before he called me.

John was so excited about his game yesterday. He was part of a triple play, and his team won. John ate what was left of my lunch – almost all of it since I am not hungry. I told him that he looked taller and that he should stay for dinner, so he can grow more. Kelly didn't want any food since she apparently worries about her weight. I know it is a serious concern with girls. Kelly is perfect, but she wouldn't listen to me if I said it.

I know that her bigger fear is that she will suffer my fate. Since my surgery, she has asked lots of questions about breast cancer and signs and symptoms and what to look for, so she catches it early. I told her that she should let her future doctor know about my history but that she should live her life. Sometimes, I think that she is angry with me for causing her to worry about her breasts before she uses them for anything. Maybe it's my own well-developed sense of guilt, but I sometimes fear that I will pass this curse on to her because of my selfish desire to have children. The warning signs were flashing when my mother was diagnosed, but I was young and stupid and didn't worry about the future. Great. Something else to feel bad about.

Bill arrived at about 6:00 to take the children home. He had been busy during the day "researching." He left me some brochures and pamphlets and

*told me that he would be back early in the morning to plan "the trip." I kissed*
*him goodbye and wondered how many more times I would be able to do that.*

# June 8

Kelly and I went to see Mom today. We asked Dad if we could take the train, and I was amazed he said "yes." I thought that he would lecture us about the dangers of trains, child molesters, drugs, and pigeons with diseases. Instead, he said he had some stuff to do and would drive us home.

It was weird riding the train with just Kelly. There were different kinds of people on the train. There were men wearing suits and some high school students. There was a guy with long hair and a bike. Dad would be annoyed if he saw that. He would probably say something like, "If he has a bike, why does he need to ride a train?"

When we got to Mom's room, it was lunch time. She said she wasn't hungry, so I ate most of her lunch. I told her about my triple play and how Dad just kept talking about it. Kelly didn't want to eat anything because she didn't want to get fat. She is built like a pencil, so I don't think she should worry. She is flatter than most of the girls in my class, so I don't think that she has to worry about getting sick like Mom.

We spent the afternoon watching TV with Mom. She made fun of a lot of the shows and commercials. She said she knew some of the lawyers in the ads. We were laughing about one of the lawyers who was fat and bald (and smelled bad, too, according to Mom) when Dad showed up. He said he was happy to hear laughter.

# JUNE 9

*I am wearing the mask most of the time now. The pneumonia isn't getting better or worse, so is that good or bad? Probably bad.*

*Last night, I looked through the reading material that Bill had brought me. I had asked him to get me brochures on cemeteries, so we could choose a place for us. He was really not happy about the assignment, but he knew that it made sense. He said that since I never let him choose anything – where to go on vacation, which hotel to stay at on vacation, which car to buy, what night to... – he might as well let me go out on a winning streak.*

*There were several places near our home. They all looked peaceful ("Because the residents are dead," Bill pointed out) and pretty. The cemetery where my parents were buried was almost an hour away, and Bill didn't want me there. He said that he would feel obligated to visit them, too, and he knew that my dad would get tired of him. I finally chose the one closest to our house. Bill said that he knew that I would do that because it was the most practical and least expensive. He had put down a deposit on two plots yesterday afternoon. He even had a picture of the ground if I wanted to see it. It was weird looking at my own grave, but I liked the adjacent trees and it was next to the exit to the road.*

*"My Dad would like the convenient parking," I joked to Bill.*

*"Maybe he can visit on Halloween. I'll leave jellybeans on your stone," Bill said in a tone that suggested that he probably will do it.*

# June 9

I was really mad at Dad today. I saw that he had papers about ceme-teries in his car. Dad plays stupid jokes. I know Mom would be really angry if she knew about it. She seemed better yesterday. I think she seemed better. I don't know how she is supposed to feel.

# JUNE 10

*I never thought that I could shiver and sweat at the same time. The infection is worse. The pneumonia is worse. The drugs are pretty good, so I'm not in pain.*

*Today, I picked out my headstone and planned my funeral. If I left those details up to Bill, I might have an obelisk, and the funeral might be capped off with a moon bounce and pony rides ("There are children coming, you know.").*

*I decided on a simple gray granite stone with a carving of the Virgin Mary on it. I was going to choose marble, but I decided that I didn't want my gravestone to be nicer than my kitchen counter. Bill said that he liked it, but if he changed his mind, he would have a different one mounted at the other end of the grave just to annoy me. He said that it might be 10 feet tall and shoot off fireworks at sunset. John would like that.*

*For the funeral, I decided that I wanted Father Mike. He had married us and baptized the children. It seemed appropriate that I finish things with him standing at the front of the church. Bill said that he would call Father Mike and see what days he had available next year. I said it might be sooner than that.*

*"I know," he sighed.*

*I told Bill that I wanted to wear the dress that I wore to Mary's wedding last year. Even though I was sick, I looked and felt pretty good that day. Bill promised to remember. I know that he will – but I did send an e-mail to Uncle*

*Jack, my secretary, and Mr. Jones at the funeral home to steer Bill in that direction when he forgets.*

*Finally, I told him that my address book was in the drawer next to my bed. I said that everybody was welcome but I didn't know if everybody could make it. He promised me that his secretary would be there as long as she could take the full day off.*

*After I selected the music, Bill told me that he was going to eat dinner in the hospital cafeteria and would then spend the night in my room. I asked him if he thought that he was being a little presumptuous that I wanted him to stay. He replied that if I didn't want him, the nurses might. I didn't want to tell him that those movies aren't real. It was nice to have him beside me, even if I was in the bed, and he was in a chair.*

# JUNE 10

I watched Abby Taylor's playoff game. Kelly teased me and asked me how my "girlfriend" played. I told her that I just wanted to see who won because Dad said that we are going to have to beat one of the teams if we want to win the championship. Her team won because she pitched almost the entire game and hit a homerun. I was happy for her, but it would have been better for us if her team lost. Dad said, "If you want to be the best you have to beat the best." That is stupid. I just want to win.

# JUNE 11

*I woke up several times in the middle of the night. Bill was sleeping soundly. I'm on a morphine drip for the pain and can't sleep. My husband is in a chair at a 45-degree angle with his shoes on, and he is sleeping like a baby. Incredible.*

*I had trouble concentrating on what Bill was saying today. Bill said that I haven't listened to him for more than 20 years, and it would be a waste of time to start now. Funny to the end.*

*Jack stopped by and said something. I'm not sure what. Still very cold. I held hands with Bill and just closed my eyes. Bill stayed all day. Run it out, Bill.*

# JUNE 11

Dad did not come to my game today. I said that I understood, but I did not. He spends all day with Mom. She sleeps a lot. Why does he need to be there to watch her sleep?

We won 7-1. I pitched four scoreless innings. I had three hits, including a triple to score the winning run. Some of the moms on the team asked how Mom is doing. I just said that she is still in the hospital. I don't really know how she is doing. They should ask Dad and then tell me.

# JUNE 12

*Exhausted. Every four hours, the respiratory therapist comes in to adjust the oxygen mask and medication levels. Bill always follows him out of the room and then returns after a few minutes, looking like he is pretending that things are getting better. I know they are not. I keep falling asleep, and when I wake up, I have to check to see if I'm still alive. I can't imagine that Heaven has this many tubes and machines, so I assume that I am alive. Hell might have this much technology, but I don't think that I was bad enough to go there – I did avoid the walk of shame by ten minutes.*

*John and Kelly came to see me today. I spoke to each of them alone. John came in first because he always wants to beat Kelly, even if it is a race to speak to his dying mother. He seemed very calm. I know that he understands that I am very sick, but I don't think he believes that I will die. I wish that that I could be 12 again.*

*John told me that he won his second play-off game yesterday. He said that he really missed having me at the game. I think that he felt a little guilty playing baseball when I am so sick. I am so happy that he has something fun to do during these days. I made sure that he understood that I want him to play hard and do his best. I wish that I could play baseball instead of lie here.*

*I told John that I have always been proud of him and that he always makes me laugh. I told him to help Dad and Kelly. He said that he would, and I believe him. Well, maybe about helping Bill.*

*Kelly came in next. She said something about clothes or a dance or a boy or a boy wearing clothes at a dance (damn medicines make it hard to concentrate). She is three years older than John, and those three years have removed the doubt about my future that protects John. She knows. She didn't have much to say because I think she wanted me to give her wisdom or life lessons. I don't have any brilliant lessons to teach, and Dr. Jacobs never gave me the book on what to tell your children before you die. I could have told her that life is not fair and that living a good life guarantees nothing. I knew a girl in college who did cocaine and every boy that said hello to her. I'm dying, and she just finished her third triathlon (and second stay in rehab).*

*I did tell Kelly that she needs to find what makes her happy and not worry about what other people think (subject to moderation and the criminal code). I told her that her father was not perfect, but he was perfect for me. She will meet handsome men and wealthy men. I told her to marry the man who makes her laugh (I hope that he is handsome and wealthy, too). She told me that she was scared. I asked her to take care of John and Bill. I think John is pretty much on his own.*

*Bill came back to the hospital after he drove the children home. I thanked him for bringing them to me. I expected him to say something like, "I wanted them to understand that life is filled with difficult moments that you have to face." Instead, he just held my hand. There is nothing left to say.*

# JUNE 12

Kelly and I visited Mom today. I was so excited to tell her about our play-off win. I think that it made her feel a little better. She told me that I make her laugh. She is proud of me. I don't know what I have done that she is proud about. Maybe it is my pitching. She looked really sick. Mom said that I should take care of Kelly and Dad. What am I supposed to do? They are older than me. Sometimes I think Mom is not coming home. I try not to think about it.

# JUNE 13

*Eggplant parmesan.*

# JUNE 13

Dad has been at the hospital since yesterday. He only came home this morning to make certain that Kelly and I were eating and ready for school tomorrow. He told me that Uncle Jack will be staying in our house for the next few days. I am glad to hear that since he usually lets me stay up late.

Dad said Mom has been asleep all day. He doesn't know if she is going to wake up again. I think I know what that means, and I hate it.

## JUNE 14

## JUNE 14

Dad didn't come home until after dinner. He didn't speak very much. Kelly asked him if she could see Mom. He said that Mom is not awake, and she wouldn't know that Kelly is there. Kelly asked why he was going back to the hospital instead of staying home with us. Then she went to her room and slammed the door. Dad looked really angry, but he didn't say anything.

I don't want to see Mom in the hospital again. I hate that place. Mom hates it, too.

# JUNE 15

Mom died today. We won 5-3. Dad woke me up this morning. He looked sad. His eyes were red like he had been crying. I had looked like that after we lost to the Yankees a few weeks ago – that pitch was a strike but the stupid umpire called it a ball and the winning run walked in. I think Andrew knows it was a strike because he won't talk about that game.

Dad told me and Kelly that Mom had died in the middle of the night. It was very peaceful, and she was not in pain. Dad said that Mom went to the funeral home, so she can get ready. I guess that she will have to look pretty since a lot of people are going to come see her. Mom had a lot of friends, especially when she started to get skinny. Maybe people like skinny women more.

I went to the game with Uncle Jack. Dad said that Mom wanted me to play in the game and that she would be able to watch me from Heaven. There was only one cloud in the sky during the game, so I guess that was hers. We won the game when the Phillies had the bases loaded. With two outs, I caught a line drive for the third out. Dad said Mom must have lifted me a little higher to get it, but she was never really that strong. She hadn't picked me up since her surgery.

Coach Kraft let me bat first. He never did that before. I had two hits. The team was pretty normal – except for the ones who talked to their parents first. Those kids said, "I'm sorry about your mom." It felt weird since nobody says they are sorry about anything during a game – especially not Doug after he dropped the ball at first and made us lose our first game. Lots of parents hugged me. That was weird, too, but it was okay.

I feel sad. Kelly is sad, too, I think but she just sits in her room.

Dad said we can see Mom tomorrow. I hope she doesn't look sick anymore.

# *June 15*

*I didn't know that Jen was keeping this journal. I just found it when I was going through the drawer by her bed at the hospital. Jen won't be writing any more. She is the lucky one. Her suffering is over, and mine is unimaginable. Dr. Jacobs was there when Jen died. I don't remember who else was there. Probably some nurse. The nurses were always there for her. They really seemed to care.*

*I guess that it is better that I didn't know that she was writing about the last few months. I probably would have tried to suggest things to her to write about or edit her words. She was better at writing. And parenting. And law. Everything, really. I don't know how to get through the next few days, and there is nobody to ask. I don't think that "Burying Your wife for Dummies" is at the book store.*

# JUNE 16

I saw Mom today at the funeral home. She was in her coffin. Dad said that there will be a viewing tomorrow for all of her friends and our family. I don't feel like writing anything else today.

# *JUNE 16*

*Jen was placed in her coffin today. I bought one that was more expensive than the one she would have chosen. I always bought the more expensive choice when she sent me shopping. It didn't matter if it was butter, gasoline, cheese, or paint. I guess I won that argument. It doesn't make me feel any better.*

# JUNE 17

Mom looked pretty today. The funeral home had two big rooms with lots of chairs and tissue boxes. Mom got the bigger room because Dad said a lot of people were coming to see her. I looked in the other room and saw an old dead guy. He didn't have as many visitors, but he did have some flowers by his coffin, so I guess he liked flowers. Mom had more.

A lot of my friends came to the funeral home with their parents. They told me that they were sorry and looked really nervous. Most of their moms hugged me. Abby came, too. She wore a dress. I don't think I ever saw her in a dress. She looked nice. She knelt next to Mom's coffin and said a prayer. She hugged me before she left. It was longer than my other friends did. It was okay.

Mom didn't look sick. She wore the dress that she wore to my cousin Mary's wedding last year. Dad said she looked beautiful. I thought that she looked dead, but not in a scary way.

Kelly looked sick the whole time. She looked like she wanted to cry, but her eyes were empty since she cried all last night. Kelly was definitely scarier than Mom.

Uncle Jack kept leaving the room and walking outside. I never saw him act so quiet. He usually told stupid jokes and made gross noises. Mom used to yell at him about it before she started laughing. I don't think grown-ups know how to act around dead people.

Father Mike came after dinner and said some prayers. It was boring, but I guess that is what people like at wakes. He said some nice things about us and asked everybody to pray for us and for Mom. Since she is dead, I think they should spend more time on us.

Dad stood close to the coffin all day. People came up and said they were sorry and asked if they could do anything to help. He said thank you a lot. He was talking but seemed to not really be there. It was weird, but I didn't say anything about it.

This is really hard on him. Kelly and I get to cry or leave the room or sit outside, but he has to stay with Mom. I don't know how he is going to leave her tomorrow. Maybe they should just bury her when we go to sleep, so he can wake up with her already gone.

# JUNE 17

*Day 3 of the Nightmare. Jen looked beautiful today. She wore that dress that she wore to a wedding last year. She told me that she wanted to wear that dress, and I actually remembered. She would probably be amazed since she never thought that I listened. Sometimes, she was right.*

*I spent the entire time at the funeral home standing by her side. I don't know how I did it. I guess you do what you have to do. I should tell that to John. He likes my "Dad Lessons."*

*I kept looking at Jen. She looked like she was sleeping. I always used to watch her before she woke up in the morning. She was peaceful then and didn't seem annoyed with me yet. Then, I usually ruined it by grabbing her breasts. I couldn't help myself. I didn't realize that I was holding what would kill her.*

*I never knew that Jen had so many friends. She must have mentioned them during one of those times I should have been listening to her. Father Mike told me that the line outside the funeral home stretched around the block. At least the viewing only lasted one night. After the first hundred people say-*

*ing, "I'm so sorry. Let me know if I can do anything," it gets exhausting. I wanted to say, "If you can't put my heart back in my chest, I don't need you." Jen would have been angry if I said it, so I let it go.*

*I was proud of John and Kelly. They are doing better than I am. I have to be strong for them, but I don't know who is going to be strong for me. That was Jen's job, and she quit on me. I know that she didn't want to die, but I am still angry.*

# June 18

Mom was buried today. I got to ride in a limo, but Dad wouldn't let us turn on the TV in the back seat. He said it was inappropriate. I think that is his favorite word.

We had to meet Mom at the funeral home. Father Mike said some more prayers, and then we left with Uncle Jack to wait in the limo. I know that he would have let me watch the TV, but Dad probably got to him first. Uncle Jack said that Dad was saying goodbye to Mom before they closed the lid. Dad did not want me and Kelly to see it. I don't know why Dad wanted to see it, either, but I don't try to understand him too much.

The Mass was Mass. Father Mike said some stuff about how good Mom was and how she loved so many people and how so many people loved her. Kelly lost it a couple times, but she did that when Mom was alive, too.

Dad spoke, too. He talked about how he met Mom and told a funny story about how she didn't want to date him when he met her. He told how he paid Uncle Jack $15 to get him to say something nice to her about him. Everybody laughed when he said it was his best investment ever. He said some more stuff about Mom and how much Mom loved us. It felt weird because people were looking at us. And looking at us. Dad looked like he was going to cry again, but he did a good job and finished up. Dad came back to his seat and looked far away again.

The limo took us to Mom's grave. It was sort of like a parade with all the cars following us. Mom's coffin was in the car in front of us, but I tried not to look at it through the window in the back of the hearse.

At the grave, more prayers. There were a lot of people crying because it was sad to think that Mom was going in the ground. Kelly couldn't watch the coffin go down the hole. I stood next to Dad the whole time. He kept holding my shoulder. He squeezed too hard, but I could take it. Mom would have told me to help Dad, so I stood there. I didn't want to hang out with Kelly anyway.

After we left the grave, we had lunch at Mom's favorite restaurant. She always ordered eggplant parmesan. Dad would get mad because she read the menu forever and then made the same choice. Dad always got the same thing, too, but he hated restaurants and wasted no time. I could hear people telling stories about Mom. I liked listening to them. Mom would have enjoyed the lunch if she wasn't dead. We have the Championship game tomorrow. I wish Mom could watch it, but I bet she would secretly cheer for Abby Taylor. Girls stick together. I hope Dad coaches first base. He lets me steal second. Sometimes.

# JUNE 18

*We buried Jen today. It seemed like it was happening to somebody else's family because I still can't believe it is happening to mine. Her coffin was placed at the front of the church before the Mass started. She was in the place where her father stopped before our wedding and handed her off to me. I didn't know that I would be letting her go on the same spot 20 years later.*

*Father Mike said very nice things about Jen and our family. She would have liked the eulogy, especially if it was about somebody else. Then it was my turn. For some reason, people expect the person who is suffer-*

*ing the most to entertain them. I think I said some of the things that I wrote down:*

"I met Jen on the first day of law school. She knew my brother from college. Jack told me that I should introduce myself to her as his brother. After I introduced myself, she didn't speak to me again for a week. Jack didn't tell me that he had dated her roommate in college, and it didn't end well. I paid Jack $15 to tell her that I was nothing like him. It worked. We started dating. I never left her side. Three days ago, she left mine. Before she left, she made certain to bless me with two wonderful children..."

*On the way to the cemetery, John wanted to watch TV in the limo. I told him that there was no way he could do that because it was inappropriate. I was probably too harsh. I need to back off on the "Dad Lessons."*

*At the grave, there were prayers and then the final goodbye. I said goodbye privately at the funeral home. I made John and Kelly leave before they closed the lid on Jen. I probably should have left, too. I wanted to see her face as long as possible. Seeing the shadow cross her face as the lid came down was a punch in the heart – or where my heart used to be.*

*After the funeral, we had lunch at Jen's favorite restaurant. It used to drive me crazy that everybody, including the waitress, knew that she was ordering eggplant parmesan. Jen studied the menu like it was a Supreme Court decision before she finally ordered it. If only I could have that time back. I wouldn't complain. Well, maybe a little.*

*When we left the restaurant, we went back to the house. I almost said "home," but it doesn't feel like home without her.*

# JUNE 19

Champions! We won 9-8. I pitched the last two innings, and I did not give up any runs. I struck out Abby to end the game. I had three hits, including a home run. It was a really great game, even though Jason gave up four runs in one inning. Jason really thinks he is great, so maybe it will be good for him to get knocked around. Dad let me steal two bases. Dad let everybody steal bases. I don't think he was paying too much attention during the game.

After the game, Dad put some dirt from the pitcher's mound in a plastic bag, so I would have a "treasure" from the game. Then we went to get ice cream. He kept saying, "You had a great game." He repeated it a lot. He didn't say much else.

Kelly stayed home. Kelly almost never comes to my games, so I guess that wasn't too different than when Mom was alive. It seems like it was more than four days ago that she died. I didn't see her very often in May and June since she was in the hospital twice. I sort of got used to her not being home. I wish that she was here. She would have said that she was proud of me, but she would not have said it every 10 minutes like Dad.